STRANGE WATERS

Jackie Taylor

ARACHNE PRESS

First published in UK 2021 by Arachne Press Limited
100 Grierson Road, London SE23 1NX
www.arachnepress.com
© Jackie Taylor 2021
ISBNs
Print 978-1-913665-36-4
ePub 978-1-913665-37-1
Mobi/kindle 978-1-913665-38-8
Audio 978-1-913665-39-5

Thanks to Muireann Grealy for her proofing.
Thanks to Kevin Threlfall for his cover design.
Printed on wood-free paper in the UK by TJ Books, Padstow.

The publication of this book is supported using public funding by the National Lottery through Arts Council England.

Acknowledgements

The Things We Can't Say originally published in Scryfa vol. 8. www.scryfa.com

An earlier version of *Rewilding* originally published in *Tymes Goe By Turnes, Solstice Shorts Festival 2020*, Arachne Press.

STRANGE WATERS

That's the thing about selkies —
they spend their lives looking out to sea
thinking about other places they'd rather be

CONTENTS

NEW LYONESSE
September 2032

Willkommen, bienvenue, welcome. Welcome, all, to New Lyonesse. My name is Chloe, I'm the caretaker here, and I'll be your guide today. You're in safe hands, I promise you. I've lived here all my life, so I know everything there is to know about this place and what happened here. We're not full, so please – spread out, get comfortable, fasten your life jackets and enjoy the tour. Just one health and safety note: please keep your hands inside the boat.

Have you been here before? Summer holidays in a caravan, or a short break in a B&B? Let's have a show of hands… that's most of you – great – so I don't need to tell you how it looked harbourside before the flood. Thanks for coming back to see us, it's wonderful to be welcoming old friends and new. It's been quiet here for so long. You'll already have noticed how changed we are.

I'll point out anything of interest as we go. We won't be going far offshore, but you'll see plenty of bird life – cormorants, oyster catchers, guillemots, terns. Puffins? Possibly, I'll call out if I see – puffins are always smaller than people imagine, they always look so big in photographs. The last couple of days there's been a pod of harbour porpoise checking us out. Very exciting, so fingers crossed. There's a colony of seals on the far side of the bay; one of them usually comes over to say hello.

You're lucky, this is a great day to visit. The tide's fairly low and the water's clear, not much run-off from the fields inland, so you should be able to get a good view down to the streets and the buildings below. As we make our way over the old village, you'll see things just breaking through the surface – like there, to the left – that cormorant stretching out its wings – that's the roof of the old Harbour Master's Office he's perched on. Below you now, can you see the outline of the car park that used to sit behind the dunes? Those black sticks are parking meters – an excellent habitat for mussels, apparently. We are very proud that a new species of barnacle has been found, thriving inside some of the old cottages, clinging to blackened hearths and old slate floors. We have become a Mecca for scientists. We're not short of researchers, students and volunteers; our little corner of the world is being studied like you wouldn't believe. Bit late, but still, it may help somewhere else. We get our fair share of weirdos too – sceptics, deniers, preachers, activists and rebels – all with their own particular axe to grind, all giving us the benefit of their rock-solid knowledge. I'm still a resident, one of the few to stay when the managed retreat from this coastline became a rout. All of us who were here have our experience and expertise.

You should be able to see the row of coastguards' cottages, curtains at the glassless windows, breathing in and out with the tide. Kelp has rooted around all the chimney pots. My grandfather lived in one of those, the one second from the end. Beautiful isn't it, when you look down? Can you see it now? We lived there when I was young; I wanted to be a mermaid then.

Is everyone OK? If you've got any questions – please – ask as we go along.

Quiet? Yes, surprising isn't it? The seagulls have all moved inland where there are richer pickings to be had.

So I guess you all know the story? Anyone not? You remember something on the TV once? OK… right. Yes, things tend to get a bit mixed up. Tragedies accumulate until they join up into one big blur, don't they?

It was on the news a lot, and after, there were documentaries, official and unofficial enquiries, a public hearing with legal representatives. Lots of time and money was spent trying to lay the blame. All the reports started off by referring to us as a 'tight-knit' community and I suppose we were – I've never lived anywhere else, so I've nothing to compare.

Hard to credit now, but it was so busy down here, specially in summer. In and out with the tide – trawlers, trips round the bay, fishing charters – we used to watch the visitors coming back after a day's mackerel fishing, chugging back into the harbour and most of the men looking green round the gills. Could have been seasickness, or could have been something to do with the crates of beer in the hold, I couldn't possibly comment.

There's wasn't much down in the old village itself, the lanes weren't designed for more than a horse and cart, so no cars, except the ones that followed their SatNavs past all the 'no vehicle' signs and got themselves well and truly stuck. There was a pub, a chapel and a corner shop, a hairdresser, and a pasty shop. A couple of summer-only cafés. The fishermen's cottages look idyllic, but no one wanted to live in them. Fine for a summer holiday, but damp, and tiny. That's why we didn't lose more lives, most of the cottages being holiday lets or second homes. Up on the hill as you drove in, that's all unchanged. The estate, a few more shops, the community centre, but it's not like it was. The heart's gone out of the place, as you'd expect. Not many people want to live on the outskirts of New Lyonesse.

There was never much work, but we were all kept busy when the summer crowds swept through. Difficult in winter, but we got by, and made enough to keep our heads above the sea. It wasn't idyllic, far from, hindsight always lends a rosy glow.

That spring, it rained day after day after day, relentless, a thirty-day monsoon. The fields were as saturated as sponges, the streams dirt-brown; you can't hold water back, we all know that. The cliffs started to crumble like fruitcake, and were washed away by run-off and undermined from the base by wind-driven seas. At the Ship, they ran a 'build an ark' competition. It was supposed to be a joke, an attempt to look on a brighter side. Then the rain stopped, but the damage had been done.

You could say we should have seen it coming. We planned, to some extent, but no one ever thought the worst would happen. It was strange; a few days before the flood, a fin whale beached, just up the coast. People seemed drawn to it, as if it were an omen; they gathered around and tried so hard to save it. Then the storm, and once the harbour wall was breached, it was all over in an hour or two. Three dead; one of them was a local girl, the others were day trippers just passing through. The council is building a memorial, up on the cliff – bit late, we all feel, but that's another story – you probably passed the site on your drive in.

Please – feel free to ask…

Is that it? Well, yes, it is.

You thought there'd be more to see? We realise there's not much here – not yet – that's why we've kept our entrance fees so low. But we have great plans for New Lyonesse.

We're very excited to share with you some of the opportunities that we're considering; most are at the feasibility stage, but we are hopeful. There's a girl who harvests dulse for all the top London chefs. She's talking about a seafood cookery school, and, if it's successful, accommodation – five star – with a boutique Wellness Spa. We've put in for funding for a glass-bottomed boat, and a kayak launch built around the chapel roof. There's some talk of a dolphin experience and possibly a *Son et Lumière,* to support our conservation goals.

Pie in the sky?

Possibly, but we have to dream.

Personally, I'd like to commission a poet in residence – well, I'd apply! And I have been asked to plan a 'Myths and Legends of the Deep' VIP package with dinner-and-private-tour, which I'm sure will be popular with some visitors.

Of course, there's always the risk that I could be replaced by an audio guide, though who'd do the rowing, eh? Virtual reality, that's another idea, fronted by that man from *Poldark*, him with the scythe and the rippling abs. You don't know who I mean? It was a TV show – way back – but he's still alive apparently, and still popular with people of the right age.

We'll be back on dry land soon. You'll find a coffee machine just inside the shed. That's the gift shop too, I should have said.

People often ask what I did here, before the flood. Like most of us from the village – a bit of this and a bit of that, cleaning, bar work, that sort of thing. I thought I'd move away when I was younger, but there's something about being born by the sea. It gets under your skin.

It's difficult, of course. What can I say? We make the best of what we've got.

We do rely on the public for their support. If you'd like to help us, you can do this in several different ways. You can sign up for our newsletter, or become a Friend, or a Sponsor, which gives you unlimited free entry, anytime.

I'm sorry you didn't see any seals today. Or puffins, dolphins, or porpoise. Or whales. They're out there though, isn't that an amazing thing? Knowing that those creatures are out there, whether we see them or not?

I realise it's disappointing. But the availability of wildlife is out of our control.

We're just reaching the end of our tour. Don't forget – keep an eye on our social media, we've got a presence on all the platforms, I think. We'd appreciate a review, particularly if you did enjoy the trip, and please come back. We're positive about the opportunities for growth in this, our 'Liminal Enterprise Zone'. But we do rely on you, our visitors. We need stable work in these unstable times, those of us who still try to make some sort of living here, in this new, tidal economy.

I'm sorry we didn't meet your expectations. Please direct your feedback to the management; they will be delighted to hear from you. I hope some of you at least found it slightly interesting. We try our best to tell the story, in the only way we can.

The pontoon can be slippery, please be careful as you leave the boat. Make sure you've got all your things. And don't forget to tell your friends. We've got great plans for New Lyonesse.

FINISTERRE
November 2032

It's Grace's job to keep everyone safe, to steady the land, to stop it falling away. She does this by building piles of stones, accumulating more each day, adding their anchoring weight around the shoreline. Grace tells herself this will save them all. She knows it's probably not true, but she can't afford to take the risk.

Her cottage squats on an outcrop of granite. This is Finisterre, the end of the world, a thin finger of land surrounded by sea. It's about to break free, weightless, honeycombed out. It will float away on the Atlantic waves unless she intervenes. There's no such thing as solid ground here. It's riddled, like woodworm. Abandoned mine shafts drop straight down, then turn and disappear out under the seabed. There are hundreds of miles of tunnels, unmapped. The earth is like Swiss cheese; just thinking about it makes her sick.

Grace has been awake through the night, listening to the wind, and counting. The storm wasn't bad, but before opening the curtains, just to be sure, she takes extra care with the things she needs to do. Everything looks the same as it was, but she can never really know for certain and once doubt starts to insinuate itself into her mind, there's no stopping its progress or moving it to one side.

This morning, the same as every morning, she must prepare to go to her stones. It takes her a long time to get ready, there are so many conversations she needs to have with herself, and so many things that have to be done. Somehow, it's nearly three o'clock by the time she leaves the cottage, and the day is almost lost to winter dusk.

Her route takes her along the lane past the Spar. A woman parks in the small, gravelled car park and picks her way through puddles to reach the shop door just as Grace passes. The woman smiles, says hello; Grace nods without lifting her head. The shop door opens and releases the smells of kerosene and last autumn's apples.

The woman behind the till says to her customer, new to the village *You've met Grace then? You mustn't mind her if she doesn't say hello. She's eighty if she's a day, and harmless enough. Buys the same number of things each time she comes in, packs them in separate bags that she brings from home. No wonder she always looks exhausted. Poor woman. Used to have the hairdressers, down by the harbour.*

The customer gives an encouraging smile; she's keen to learn who's who in the community but doesn't what to seem too inquisitive. The woman behind the till continues quietly, almost to her herself; the customer has to lean in towards her to hear.

She was always a bit alternative. Then after the flood… she lost her granddaughter. Lovely girl. Gilly. Grace has never been the same.

Grace reaches the footpath that only she uses, the way narrowed by gorse, bramble and blackthorn. She clambers over boulders scarred with lichen. Beware adders, they say, basking in the summer sunshine. But not today. It's wet and windy. Stormy, but not bad for here. The fields are like brown corduroy, frayed at the sea-edges. The land has been gulped away by the sea, greedy mouthfuls at a time. *Beware – Mine Workings – Keep Out – Danger.* New shafts tend to open after rain.

She sings to herself as she hurries along, children's songs mostly, simple but enough to block out the voice that wants to tell her that she's too late. She crosses the abandoned road that used to lead down to the drowned village. This is her greatest burden; she failed to protect this place and those people.

*

Banjo and Wes are parked up in a lay-by on the road overlooking the sea. Below them is the road that leads down to where the old village used to hunker, before the harbour wall was breached. The road stops abruptly now with fencing and 'keep out' signs. The cab of the pick-up smells of sheep dog and pasties. Condensation drips on them, despite the slip-opened windows. They've been yarning all afternoon. It's been too wet to work, much better to sit tight and put the world to rights. Grace crosses the road in front of them, unmistakable in her wet-weather gear and her focus.

Wes says *There she goes again. What a life she's had. Daughter died in childbirth, then losing the granddaughter in the flood.*

And Banjo says *She used to have the hairdressers, remember? Cut my Pauline's hair for years.*

And they both nod slowly at this, like a pair of dashboard dogs, and Wes remembers what a looker she'd been back in the day, despite being a bit of a hippy-type, although you'd never believe it now.

Panicked by the memory of the village and the people she couldn't save, Grace crosses the road and picks up the footpath again, and starts running, sort-of, slipping often. Every day this is becoming harder; she never used to be this late. The rain on her face is slimy and the wind is pushing her back, but at last she reaches the rocks. She looks over the edge. Way down below her, an arc of pale gold sand, a stream cutting through it, taking fresh water to the salt waves. Off to the east, she can hear the clamour from the guillemot cliffs. The birds cram together on vertiginous ledges; the chicks are just three weeks old when they dive to the sea. She wishes they would all stay in the safety of their nests forever.

She crosses the granite bridge over the zawn, the sea below scouring the base of the cliffs. The plateau is creviced and cracked, with sea on three sides. Here are her stones, her beautiful, orderly field of stones. Pile after pile of pebbles, like the cityscape of an alien world. There are three stones on the base of each cairn, another three in the gaps to make the next layer, one larger stone over the top.

She looks around the stone field, trying to decide where to build today's cairn. The stones are so well-known to her that they feel almost like friends or family. Strangers sometimes add their own small monuments to hers as they walk past on the coast path. Grace doesn't mind this, as long as it is done in a way that's respectful.

She is only too aware of the irrationality of her actions, but this building and saving is the only thing that makes any sense for her to be doing anymore. Nearly fifty years ago, in one single day, she lost her daughter and gained a granddaughter, her beautiful, beautiful Gilly, hers to nurture and raise. And now Gilly is gone too, ten years ago. In the face of these cold, hard facts, the act of trying to save the world by piling stones around a fractured coastline is as sensible a response as any she can imagine.

In the corner of her vision, she catches sight of a kestrel, flexed into the wind. She watches, her mind quiet – captured for a few precious moments. She breathes, breathes, breathes in the peace. The kestrel wheels away, arcing into the wind with a cry like quartz.

She closes her eyes against the field of stacked stones in front of her. If she just thinks of the kestrel, can she keep the worry away? She knows it won't last, this quiet. It never does. Recalling the times she brought Gilly here after school, in the summer or on Sundays, she squeezes her eyes shut, refusing to open them to the sea-world in front of her. They used to build streets, villages and towns out of pebbles, decorated with ropes of purple seaweed, white cuttlefish bones, candy floss coloured shells and feathers. It was their favourite game, so much better than sandcastles that collapsed and disappeared with every incoming tide. After Gilly, and the flood, this game of careful construction, the process of strengthening and reinforcing, had become life and death to Grace, a daily routine that couldn't be broken. She is so tired, right down in her bones. She would like to rest now, to not be responsible for saving the rest of the world. She wants the kestrel overhead, just the kestrel, and quiet, simple things. She yearns for the smell and sound of the sea, and the feel of the wind, without worrying about the consequences.

Grace sits on a flat jagged slab, feeling the cold seep through layers of clothes. She is too tired to gather her stones. She is too tired to build a new cairn. She can't do it anymore, not today, perhaps never. The weight is too much for one person. She hesitates then lifts a stone from the top of a cairn, leaving it incomplete, defenceless. She holds her breath, waiting for the terrible consequences. Nothing changes. There is no shudder of earth, no shift of land. What if...? What if...? Could she really stop all this, and know that everyone would be safe? Can she take the risk?

The stone she has removed is rounded and sea-worn. It seems that she has been travelling with these sea stones all her life. It's nearly dark. She returns to the granite bridge across the zawn and drops the stone over the edge. It bounces three times on the faces of the rock, then disappears into the push and pull of the waves. A seal-shadow twists in the curl of a wave; Grace watches to see if the creature will surface to observe the shore and return the stare of anyone watching, as they normally do, but it doesn't appear, hunting deep down by the submerged rock face or arrowing back towards their rocky colony on the far side of the bay.

Before the sea encroached, there was a cove here, inaccessible on foot, where the seals hauled out, twenty or thirty at a time. Her mother would sit and watch them for hours, while Grace plaited grass, or collected sea glass or other treasures to take back to her father. Her mother was always reluctant to leave; Grace thinks she can remember her mother crying as she sat on the cliffs watching the seals.

Grace follows the path that loops and switches down to the arc of sand. Buried deep below is the old road down to the harbour, and the shop she used to own with the flat above, flooded now, like the whole village. Her mother and father had lived in the cottage at the end of the terrace, nearest the sea. Captured by a fisherman, as selkie-born women so often are, her mother had been taken into marriage, motherhood and domesticity without really knowing what was expected of her.

*

Grace has never learned to swim, fearing the sea's draw and her mother's legacy. Churning waves wash over outcrops of rock, and heave and break, and between the rocks is a quiet pool of white foam within the black of the sea, protected and circled, serene and inviting. If she lay down in the soft foam, would she float? Could she lie on her back and watch the clouds clearing, with nothing to think about except the sky quietly darkening? Could everything be reduced to a single, weightless moment?

The woman in the Spar wonders whether Grace has returned yet; she hasn't seen her go by. She decides to close up early. They used to be busy all year round with visitors, but it's so quiet now, hardly even worth opening. There's no one around except Banjo and Wes chewing the fat up the road in the lay-by. She comes out from behind the till and swaps 'open' for 'closed'.

Banjo and Wes call it a day – might as well. Weather permitting, they'll come back tomorrow and make a start on the footings for the memorial to the village that was washed away.

Wes says *We'll be lucky to find something solid to work off, it's all mine waste and shillet.*

They know how important it is that the memorial should be rock solid. No-one wants the embarrassment of a civic memorial that crumbles into the sea at the first sign of bad weather. It's taken so long to get to this point. At first, the need to navigate a community's grief meant that no decisions could be reached. The memorial carried so much meaning, but ten years on, there is an almost desperate desire to get the job finished. Then there might be a chance that everyone can move on.

Over the cliff, a kestrel hovers, flexed into the wind and watchful. A slow arc, a cry like quartz, and fresh water mingling with salt. Grace watches and tries to think of nothing, except the sky quietly darkening above her.

Name
Chloe Bolitho
Position You Are Applying For
General assistant (zero hours). Meadow Care Home.

Chloe Bolitho is finding it hard to summon up the particular kind of bright and shiny language that's needed to complete a job application. It doesn't help that she's sitting on a bench on the harbour wall to do it. The sea is jade green and it's wintry, but not in a colour supplement, mugs of hot chocolate, rugs and cable-knit jumper kind of a way. This is Cornwall, and it's mizzly, but not particularly cold. Droplets are settling like snow globes all over her fleece, but she's not getting rain-soaked, just progressively damper.

She spends a lot of time down by the harbour. She comes here when she wants to think. It's not a random thing; there's a family connection. Chloe Bolitho is sitting on her dad, or on his bench, to be exact, leaning against the gold-paint lettering: *Forever in our hearts. He loved this view,* except he hadn't loved, or even particularly liked, this view. Much as he loved being on the boats, the sea was just the sea, a place of work for him, cold, unforgiving, dangerous at times. He could never understand why people were so keen to come down on holiday when they could fly off to somewhere hot, somewhere with a bit more life than here.

When someone dies, you have to make all sorts of unexpected decisions that you aren't prepared for. All the granite memorial benches are identical, lined up along the harbour wall and looking straight out past the island towards Eddystone. When Chloe and her mum were choosing the words, they didn't know what to put. The word count was pretty low for an entire life. All the other inscriptions seemed to mention the view, so they did too. It seemed rude not to.

Where do you see yourself in five years' time?
Are you kidding me?

She chews the end of her pen. How is she supposed to imagine five years into the future when she can't even think about tomorrow? Right here, right now, she's trying to be mindful and present in the moment, as she has been advised.

So, where do you see yourself in five years' time?
Fuck knows.

Chloe Bolitho strikes a match and lets it burn until she feels the shock of it on her fingertips. She always carries a box of matches, even though she doesn't smoke anymore. Back in school, she'd conscientiously taken to smoking as part of her career strategy. She'd wanted to be a poet when she grew up, and to that end her action plan included the development of a gravelly rasp and dressing like a cool, unhealthy, old school Goth. She still wants to be a poet, but she's completely over the need to kill herself by smoking. She can't afford it anyway, but she still likes fire.

Previous Experience
Here goes –
Bar work, cleaning, dog walking, dog grooming, front of house, back of house, delivering pizza – Chloe Bolitho has

done it all, and more besides. She was a kitchen porter for a while, all sudded up, and a sous-chef, but she didn't really have the skills. She's run a short-order grill, but all she got was cash in hand and hair that stank of dirty fries.

Like most people round here, Chloe Bolitho turns her hand to anything. There's a bit of work out of season, better than most seaside towns. She can always pick up a few hours in the Spar, or behind the bar in the Ship, split shifts, but that's just the way it is.

Most of her old school friends are away at Uni now. They come back for the holidays and expect to pick up the cream of the seasonal jobs. She doesn't really hang out with them anymore. She misses the way they used to be together, but they look down on her for staying put – not that they say anything, but there are silences, the really shitty kind of long silences between people who should be able to pick up from where they were, but can't. They come into the pub and she listens to their plans, bemused by their confidence in the future and their cast-iron certainties.

Chloe and her mates used to come down to the harbour wall after school to smoke and drink, messing around on the strip of concrete between land and sea. They called it Death Row: dead people's benches decorated with trite inscriptions and brittle, faded, plastic flowers. She didn't know any better then.

Please explain any gaps in your CV. Is there anything else about you that we should know?
No.
So – where do you see yourself...?
...in five years' time? OK, seeing that you insist...

It's hard to voice, and she's never told anyone before, not even when she was dressing in black and smoking like a chimney and stealing her dad's San Miguels. It's not even relevant for this particular job, so she probably doesn't need to say anything about it. When she was younger, she wanted to be a mermaid, but now Chloe Bolitho wants to be all over YouTube, like Kae Tempest only younger. She wants to be the voice of the rural-stroke-coastal disenfranchised youth, a critically acclaimed, widely respected, relevant, authentic poet. Or poet/artist. So in five years' time, this is what she'd really like to be, except she doesn't have a clue how to get from here to there, how you get to put 'poet' or 'artist' on your CV.

Explain (briefly) why you want this position.
(max 50 words)
I need the money (4 words). Next.

Qualifications
Nothing relevant, sorry, unless dog grooming counts? And I'm good at English, if that's any help?

Her mum thinks that a qualification in Health and Social Care will be useful to fall back on. Chloe didn't sit her A levels, what with her dad being ill and then dying, and everything else as well. The school sent her home with a study plan. Everybody seemed to think it was best to leave her to work things out in her own way, as best she could.

Could you please expand?
(There are gaps in your CV which will need to be explained before we can move on to the next page)
My dad died last year, and there was other stuff.

She wonders how much they really need to know in an application for a zero-hours contract in a care home. For

25

completeness, she could tell them that there had been a baby, or at least the start of one. It was lost almost before she knew it was there; Chloe wasn't even sure how much of a baby there had been. There was some pain, but not much blood.

No name. No memorial. Just a fire, she imagines. The hospital sent her home with Co-Codamol.

Her mum said, *It's such a shame you lost the baby,* like it was a textbook or a sock. *To be honest, it's probably for the best. And let's not tell your dad, he's going through enough…*

Her dad died a month later. Although they'd expected it, she never believed it would actually happen. The school sent her home with a study plan.

Does that adequately explain the gaps?

Qualifications (in reverse order)
See attached list, and a letter from the school.

Chloe Bolitho's dad left school at 15 and he'd been a fisherman all his working life. Fishermen never learn to swim. Not worth it, they say, if you're going down, that's it, game over. He died on a trolley on the way to A&E, denied the romance of a death at sea.

Current Position
Haven't I already…?

Chloe is currently enjoying a portfolio career (bar work, dog walker, retail – see above). Her main role over the past twelve months has been caravan cleaner/housekeeper, Easter to October half term, self-employed. This season, she thought the boss would take her on the books officially, with a written contract, sick pay, holiday pay, all of that. No chance. She's still self-employed. It's a con, but she has a take it/leave it choice.

There's always someone else who wants the work.

To be a poet, Chloe Bolitho knows she'll have to move, to Bristol, or even London, and she'll need to build her brand. She suspects it'll be a good idea to change her name to something that doesn't signpost where she's from. She's not sure whether it's too soon to do the name-change thing, and anyway, she's not one hundred percent settled on a new one yet. A bit like getting a tat; best to get it right first time.

What has been your greatest challenge (in your current position). How did you overcome that challenge?
Have you ever tried cleaning a three berth caravan in an hour?

They get an hour – max – per caravan, including stripping and making up the beds. Some of the vans are plush enough, linen cushions, free wi-fi, the works. But most – Chloe goes in and they stink of damp, and when she leaves, they still stink of damp, underneath the pine-fresh Glade. The walls are plywood, paper thin. You could put your foot straight through, or your fist – it happens more often than you'd think. A lathered guest: 'It was just an accident.'

Sometimes Chloe Bolitho is tempted to put her foot through a caravan wall and blame it on a guest who's just left. Or her fist, but that might hurt or even scar. What she'd really like to do is set a match to the plywood walls. Caravans go up in a flash, she knows.

Self-motivated?
It depends.

Chloe Bolitho knows that poets do rash, poetic things. It goes with the job. Necessary personal qualities include a tendency to self-destruct. So, is this the question she should really be answering: *Chloe Bolitho – how much of a poet do you really want to be? How committed to your career path are you? Will you give it all you've got?* Chloe suspects that burning down a caravan won't cut the mustard. It would be too easy, a bit pathetic and small-town sad.

Are you a team player?
Preferably not, but thanks for asking.

Your greatest strength? (Here's a hint if you're having trouble answering: resilience, loyalty, sense of humour, pluck?)
Shouldn't you be asking if I'm kind?

She thinks they should be asking if she's caring, empathetic, good. If she can tell when someone wants a chat and a joke, or just to be left alone with their own thoughts. If she can sit at a bedside and summon bright and shiny conversation out of nowhere. If she can stroke someone's hand for hours, when there's nothing more to be done. Shouldn't these personal qualities be pre-requisites for the job?

Can we revisit where you want to be in five years' time?
You don't have to rub it in. I'm kidding myself; I know that. But why shouldn't I want to be something amazing? Why the fuck not, actually?

She shouts this out loud, and then looks around quickly to see if anyone has heard. She strokes the bench, mouths 'sorry Dad'. She can almost hear his voice: *Chloe!* Half telling her off, but half laughing at the same time.

There are days when she is submerged in grief, and can't see any way back to solid ground. There are other days when she manages to stay steadfast. Her dad's bench is her anchor. She comes here when she wants to remember. Sometimes she writes poems. She writes what she knows, like they taught her at school, and she's started to write about things she doesn't know, too. She practises saying her words out loud, making her voice bigger, sending herself out and up and over the sea.

The application form is so wet now that it's lost its will to live. The ink has run like mascara from the pound shop. She's had enough. She'll apply online when she gets home, cut and paste a suitable personal statement from some other job application. She won't mention wanting to be a poet, but her English Lang and Lit grades are there for everyone to see. A*. She thinks her dad would have been proud, but by the time her results came through, it was too late for him to say.

She gets up and stretches and takes the J-cloth out of the bag she's carrying. She wipes down the bench, as she does every week, and clears away the weeds that are pushing up through the concrete around the base.

Like her dad, she doesn't much like the view. There's sea, and sometimes it's grey, and sometimes it's blue, and sometimes jade green like today. Some days it's busy with trawlers, day-trip boats and jet skis, and on other days, wintry days like today, it's empty and flat and there's no horizon, no clear line to separate sea and sky. Chloe has no trace of sea-longing inside her, as so many others do who are born by the water. If there are any selkie shadows in her, they are deep-buried.

Chloe wonders how she would feel about a different kind of view, something other than the island and Eddystone. A view that's just a view, without memories, or loss, or guilt, or any other sort of weight.

She throws the soggy paper into the dog poo bin and climbs down the steps. The reinforcing steel rods are exposed, the concrete path crumbling, and the steps stop short, so that she has to jump down the final foot or so. Her feet sink into the pebbles as she lands, leaving land-slipped hollows as she walks towards the sea. She jumps over the strandline of twisted kelp and fishing line and picks up a length of slimy bladderwrack and bursts the bladders – not as satisfying as bubble wrap but it makes her laugh.

She thinks she'll get a tat. It'll have to be a small design, or a short word, she can't afford much. She's been thinking about the word 'Forever' in a beautiful, gothic font, on her forearm, or maybe her shoulder. Her mum will go mad. And Chloe isn't sure she's got the nerve.

Where does she wants to be in five years' time? She selects a smooth, flat pebble. It's a rich, iron red, with a seam of sharply defined white like a tiny broken spine. It fits snugly into her palm. She skims it, five perfect hops. She takes it as a sign.

PELT
May 1946

Marissa was one of those exceptions to the rule. Selkie-born, her instincts were inside-out, back to front, like a badly folded coat. Tired of freedom, she longed to be captured by a man who would take her to a home inland, far from the sea. Most women inherit something unwanted from their mothers; Marissa had a scent, and the hint of webbed skin between her ring and middle fingers, and a longing for romance that would always blindside her.

Her story was tied up and knotted in myth and misunderstanding. In the village they said that she brought bad luck, but fishermen are superstitious at the best of times, looking for ill-fortune even when their nets are full, and the seas are crystal calm. One lovelorn fisherman in desperation had followed her onto the reef, where he lost his life for her, willingly. Marissa was blamed for his stupidity. Another man, chapel-fierce and steadfast in all his ways, stoned her from the clifftop, fearful for his soul in the face of her temptation. Marissa bore a scar over her right eye until the day she died. People brought their self-born luck to her, good or ill, and she couldn't help that. But in the face of this, who could blame her for wanting to settle? Some called her mermaid, but she was never that, rather, she was an in-between selkie, inhabiting a between the tides, shoreline place. She yearned for stability. Not all selkies resist the love of a land-born man, some seek it out, desperate for a bounded, bone-dry home and hearth.

Marissa's war had been a churning of the ocean, an invasion of sea-craft. It had been harbours blocked by chains, and sand

31

dunes laced with barbed wire. It had been soldiers practicing landings and then setting off from her beaches towards the beaches of France. The war was over now, but peace had yet to become a way of life.

Marissa had watched him for weeks from her spot on the rocks before she arranged their initial meeting. He came along the beach every day, usually led on by a lumbering Labrador. The sudden changes that sparked through this solitary, beach-combing man drew Marissa's attention. He'd drag his feet through shingle and seaweed, shoulders hunched, head bent, and then suddenly break into a jog, then a sprint along the strand-line, flinging his arms wide as if heading for a finishing tape. Sometimes she watched him stand motionless, looking out to sea as the tide advanced almost to his feet, and then he'd shake as if woken, and bend to pick up stone after stone, skimming one after another in quick succession, low to the waves, like a burst of gunfire, as if to remind himself that there was still the possibility of movement and action, as if to signal that there was still a young man present underneath the overcoat of war.

*

Marissa had engineered their meeting, making a fuss of the slow, smiling Labrador, overcoming her loathing of dogs to do so. They had chatted, and they got on well, as she knew they would. She started to reorganise her shifts at the canteen so that they met up most days, purely by chance.

Samuel's war had been spent in London, as a journalist on a home desk covering bombings, fires and civilian deaths. Marissa wanted to know every detail about life in the city before and during the war, but Samuel was not to be drawn, other than to say what total, complete madness it had been. He had moved down for a while to stay with his parents. He thought he might even stay on, perhaps try to get a job on the local paper. He hinted that there'd been someone, up in London. Marissa held her tongue and didn't pry. Everyone had both a story and a history.

Samuel kept his war to himself. He hadn't managed to shed his city skin yet. He still smelled of the Blitz, air raid shelters and smoke. He smelled of nightclubs, sharp suits and black-market cigarettes. Marissa couldn't even begin to imagine his world. She lightly brushed against him on their beach walks, hoping for some of him to rub off onto her. She sent filaments across the space between them, blaming the sea winds for the waywardness of her long, grey-black hair. She allowed some of her hair-threads to remain on his clothes, embedded and proprietorial. The old Labrador growled at her.

Marissa had never been anywhere but the coast. Not yet. She suspected that Samuel would be back up to London as soon as he fathomed the limitations of seaside life. She just wanted to make sure that she went with him. She had no interest in falling in love with some fisherman and ending up half-in, half-out of the tides. She knew that the further inland she could get, the safer she'd be.

Marissa knew that a weekend away with Samuel was high-risk when they'd only known each other such a short time. But the war had changed everything, kaleidoscoping action and reaction, and fracturing consequences. A double room in a guest house had become, if not the norm, at least a course of action that wasn't totally out of the question. Marissa could picture them, like a scene from a film, sitting in a pretty tea house eating éclairs and drinking from rose-sprigged china cups, so obviously a couple, and deeply in love. People would smile at them, rejoicing at their good fortune at making it through unscathed. She could imagine Samuel's hand lying lightly over hers, he was looking into her eyes, and there was a soundtrack, not violins, but perhaps birdsong. Marissa convinced herself that this would be the best course of action; her whiskers confirmed that it was the right thing to do.

She found a guest house from an advertisement in the weekend paper and wrote for details. She received a leaflet back, promising bed, breakfast and evening meal, hot and cold running water, tea making facilities and favourable rates for commercial travellers. She requested two nights and paid extra for a private bathroom and a view. She booked their train tickets. They would be Mr and Mrs for the duration, with a signet ring moved from her right hand to her left. The photograph in the brochure was grainy and difficult to decode but the room seemed spacious and well-ordered, high-ceilinged as you'd expect from a town house, with full length windows that opened up onto one of the finest roads in the town.

Samuel had looked surprised, shocked even, when she told him about the holiday. He said, of course, he was just surprised – but yes, of course. It would be wonderful. 'You're not like the girls in London,' he said. She tried not to be upset by his remark. She wanted more than anything to be exactly like one of those girls.

In preparation for their holiday, she borrowed a cardboard suitcase, and splashed out on a permanent wave. The hairdresser showed her how to pin-curl her fringe. She bought nylons and lingerie for the first time, peach-perfect and silky against her fur.

It was her first time on a train. Samuel opened the door for her, and Marissa thought that the whole train would tumble out onto the platform it was so full – of men elbow-to-elbow in the corridors, and women laughing, and babies and children, and so much heat and body smell that she couldn't breathe and thought she was going to faint. As soon as the train pulled away and started to accelerate, the track running along the foot of the cliff parallel to the sea, she shut her eyes tight to avoid the temptation of looking. The faster the train went, the more nauseous she felt. She didn't open her eyes again until they arrived, just over two hours later. Samuel, chatting to some demobbed soldiers, didn't notice her discomfort, although one of her stray hairs on his jacket did try, without her authority, to prod him into some sort of solicitous action.

She almost stumbled when she stepped off the train, her legs weak, a headache gathering from the scar over her right eye and threatening to take hold. 'Are you alright? You look like you need a bit of fresh air,' Samuel said, and walked off towards the exit without waiting for a reply. They wandered along busy, broad streets, looking for landmarks, Marissa holding a map that seemed to be an artist's impression of any old city – museum, post office, cathedral, gardens – the sketch of each place of interest unhelpfully straddling entire neighbourhoods. Samuel didn't seem to mind being lost. Invigorated by the city streets, he strode forward, looking up at pediments and columns, admiring the solidity of the buildings. Marissa wasn't used to being surrounded by so many hard surfaces and geometries, so unlike her sculpted, sea-worn rocks. She thought she would love it here, but instead she felt heavy-limbed and awkward, perfectly out of place.

Samuel whistled as they walked. He was in his natural habitat, and as much at home and comfortable as she was uneasy, a creature out of water. Her scalp itched; her thick, grey-black hair fought against the tyranny of the new perm. She was uncomfortably hot and clammy in her new outer skin of trench coat (belted, beige), silk scarf, beret, tan leather gloves. Samuel had said when he met her at the station, 'You scrub up well!' And she'd winced at the thought of the skinning knives used to clean down pelts.

She wanted to take the trench coat off and carry it, but there was drizzle, and it was the wetting kind, and if her skin got wet, she would smell of the sea. She was never sure if anyone else could smell it, but the thought of it made her burn with shame.

Samuel turned off the main shopping street. He didn't have much luggage, just a small army satchel, slung crossways over his body, and he was wearing the same coat as he wore back home on his walks along the beach. His brown brogues were scuffed at the toe and worn down at the outer edges of the heel. Marissa followed him, trying not to be aggravated by his shoes and his whistling, which reminded her of hunting dogs and culls. Unused to heels, she struggled over uneven cobbles with her cardboard suitcase. She was never elegant, not on dry land. She couldn't help thinking that he might have offered to help with her case. She wished he would stop whistling, seeing that they were now in a proper city.

He pointed down a wide street opposite a park. She'd never seen anywhere so neat or so grand.

'I think it's down there,' Samuel said.

'Isn't this wonderful!' She smiled brightly, trying not to show her teeth. She followed his whistle, wishing she'd worn brogues herself, but that would have signalled a lack of commitment. She really had thought that Samuel would have made more of an effort. She thought the city boy would emerge; urbane, sophisticated, other.

They walked past wide steps leading up to panelled front doors with brass handles and important-sized letterboxes. They passed steep steps leading down to dark basements and tradesmen's entrances. 'How difficult can it be to find?' she said, as they paused at a corner.

A door opened, and briefly within: a tiled hallway, a mother struggling to get two little girls into coats and boots, the father reading the newspaper while he waited. The woman looked at her, and smiled, with tears in her eyes.

Marissa knew that there should be something inherently romantic about getting lost in a strange place, opening yourself up to chance encounters and experiences. But she could feel that there was no romance here, no escape route, no way out. Her intuition had let her down.

The drizzle became steady and then driving rain. Marissa had an umbrella. Samuel almost managed to hold it over her, and they walked along brushing shoulder against shoulder, but rain dripped off the points and one side of her coat was soaked. She wanted to keep moving in case the smell of the sea became unmistakably hers.

She looked up. A worker high up on the roof of one of the town houses was crouching over, hammering. A massive window had been left open, and curtains billowed out, heedless of the rain, as if happy to be released from the shackles of blackout. And on the wall opposite, at last, a sign for their guest house, the brass plaque, discreet.

Marissa had a story rehearsed and ready, and was almost disappointed that the landlady, thin and efficiently tweed-suited, didn't ask any questions. Their room was on the first floor, high-ceilinged, restrained, and impeccable. Long windows looked out over roofs and trees, layer after layer, out to the hills beyond. The bed was a stout, carved mahogany four-poster, hung with bright chintz, as if the heaviness and darkness of the past years could be erased with flowered drapery.

Marissa unlaced her shoes and climbed onto the bed. The mattress was soft and giving, and she lay back, happy to be moored in such a comfortable place. She was so used to being supported, too much earth-pull drained her muscles and her mind of energy. A damask-covered sofa guarded the foot of the bed. Samuel lay down on it, rearranging cushions.

'This'll do me fine,' he said quickly, as if to make his point before there could be any hint of misunderstanding. 'Do you mind if...?' and he took off his jacket and jumper and went into their private bathroom. She heard him turn the taps on, the water falling into the bath like a drum.

Marissa was relieved, in a way. She scratched and scratched at her scalp, cursing her newly-permed hair, and only stopping when she thought her sharp fingernails might draw blood.

At least she had been spared the necessity of explanation; the need to carefully select the right words to soften the revelation; the need to decode and decipher his first, revealing reaction to her otherness. Her body remained covered, unmolted, unseen.

Tired already of the bounded, bone-dry city, she imagined her sea-home. The almost invisible webbing between her ring and middle fingers tingled, and she licked the skin, tasting salt. Perhaps a sailor or a fisherman would suit her better; a man who understood the split in her heart. She'd inherited from her mother this understanding; that a selkie always yearns for the other place.

Her whiskers suggested that perhaps she didn't need any sort of anchor and reminded her to protect herself against that longing for romance that always blindsided her. Marissa picked up Samuel's jumper from the floor and unthreaded her hairs, and while he soaked in the bath, she brushed out the permed curls that she hated. The hair-threads that she'd encouraged to embed on his clothing, she reclaimed, putting them back to the comfort of her head.

LIFELINES
April 2010

Caro: Wednesday morning, Ferry Cottage
Three items: not much of a list, as lists go.
Pack bag ☑
Spare keys > Rosie ☑
Phone Nix ☑

Three items, all ticked off. My bag's packed; I took the spare keys up the lane to Rosie's earlier this morning; I left a message for Nix. Misdialled first time, nerves I suppose, but it's done, and I'm relieved; I was dreading it.

I didn't sleep last night, so it was a relief to walk up to Rosie's first thing to drop the keys off. She's a farmer's wife, so I knew she'd be up, and it was a distraction from worrying about what I should pack, or whether I should clear out the fridge, or anything else I might have invented to fill up this morning's waiting. The walk was a tonic. It feels like a proper spring at last, delivering all the things a proper spring should – a razor-sharp sunrise, a thin slice of mist over the valley, the spice of primroses, new shoots of wild garlic getting thuggish in the lane-banks on the approach to the farm. I'll paint the hedgerows when I get home; I'll make an attempt at capturing all the rainbow greens of spring.

I haven't packed a mirror. I know how pale and tired I look, without needing to see the evidence. There's something interesting and surprisingly subtle in the dark colours of the skin under my eyes, but I'd rather not engage with it. I seem to have lost, temporarily I hope, my forensic artist's eye, at least when it comes to examination of my own middle-aged features. Rosie, bless her, said she thought I was looking a lot better, that it was probably the relief of getting on with it after so much uncertainty and waiting. She meant well and kissed me on the cheek. She wished me luck, as if I was going into an exam.

All those times I've stood outside the main hall at exam time and said to the fidgety, hyped-up kids in the queue, *I'm not going to wish you luck because none of you need it. You'll all be fine.* They never believed me. I didn't believe me, so why should they? But it was a ritual and it made them laugh. Not proper laughing though, just the nervous kind. Rosie said she'd ring the hospital later.

Mark used to laugh when I wrote down things on my 'to do' list that I'd already done, just for the satisfaction of crossing them out again. *Phone Nix.* I'd already sorted out last year's Christmas card, with the brief, handwritten note summarising their year in a few unrevealing, cheery sentences. Her address and phone number were printed in serifed gold font on the reverse of the card, just where you'd see them when you first opened the envelope. I managed to misdial the first time – nerves – and then got her voicemail, and I'm not sure what I said, or whether it made any sense, but it's done, that's the main thing.

Nix: Thursday morning, Paddington Station.
Fifteen minutes to spare. Perfect. Guardian, wine gums, flask on the table. Handbag on the seat next to me, holdall on the seat opposite, minimising the chance of anyone joining me.

I don't remember the last time I took the train down to Cornwall. We brought the boys down on holiday by car a couple of times, when they were still young enough to enjoy buckets and spades and their parents' company. We never managed to see Caro, which is shameful thinking about it now.

The boys have probably only met their auntie once, maybe twice, at a wedding or a funeral. I don't think I've been down by train since the last time I saw her. It must be… fifteen years? Surely not.

Why did she leave that message on my voicemail? A typical Caro message – that she's going into hospital, but *don't worry.* Nothing useful like for how long, or what's wrong, or how serious it is. But she must want me to come, otherwise why call after all these years?

Dismal back gardens. Broken trampolines and discarded toys. Greenhouses without glass, ripped sofas without seats. I can't believe the mess some people live in.

I still don't know what her message meant. Will she think I'm interfering again? I only want to help, she's my sister after all. I only ever wanted to do my best for her.

Caro: Wednesday morning, Ferry Cottage
The tide's out and the morning light on the mudflats looks like the bloom on ripe grapes. The jetty on the far shore is still broken. It looks just like any other day.

Nix never saw the beauty here. For some reason she was with us the day Mark and I first visited Ferry Cottage with the estate agent, the appointment made almost as a joke, or maybe a dare. Up until then, it had just been a dream – Mark and I didn't seriously think we could afford to move down. But everything is so much easier when you're young. Both just out of college, we had nothing really to give up. Mark's parents gave us some money, or did they lend it to us? And it felt like fate. We took our good luck so much for granted. Ferry Cottage was damp, dilapidated and cheap. It was perfect. I wrote lists and lists and lists, fixing all our plans to neat, lined paper.

Nix must have been on holiday with us, that was it.

Camping. Me and Mark, her and… I can't even remember his name, the boyfriend before the one she married.

When we found Ferry Cottage, we thought all our dreams had come true. And then the accident, three weeks after we moved in. I've never taken any sort of luck, good or ill, for granted since that day.

When things were really bad, not immediately, but in the months after, I still wrote lists. Except I lost all my 'doing' words and made lists of nouns. Concrete, solid things. Boiler. Gas. Money. Things like that. Except nothing ever really got done, nothing got crossed off. They were more like clues to what real life should be. Lifelines. I think I wrote them up on the kitchen walls. It seems like something I would have done, back then.

After Mark died, Nix wanted me to go back to London with her. I couldn't do that – it would have felt like treachery. She nagged me to go into teaching, like I'd planned, and I have to admit she was right about that. Not that she'd ever understood about art. She thought it was about freedom and being irresponsible and unreliable, about not engaging with the way the real world works. She never understood the rigour, the discipline, the energy that's needed. Teaching wasn't the best thing for my own work, but I doubt whether anything else would have been more productive.

I'm sure Nix only ever tried to do her best for me. The worst thing is that I don't remember exactly what happened between us. It was during the time that I was writing lists on the walls. Now, I just want to see her again.

Nix: Thursday morning, Plymouth Express
I could have made more effort to stay in touch, but I was always so busy, getting qualified, becoming an associate, taking on my own projects, raising the boys. And when all's said and done,

she was the one who said she didn't want to see me again. I think so anyway. It was so long ago.

I've got a photo somewhere, taken outside the cottage that day they – we – first viewed it, with Mark whirling Caro round. I tried to make them see sense – how were they going to manage? But they were young and in love and we've all been in that place where you feel so charmed that you can't believe that anything bad could ever happen to you.

Caro seemed fine at first – or as fine as you can be in that situation. It was later that she fell apart. I tried to get her to come back to London, and when she wouldn't, I practically dragged her into teacher training college. I tried to help her with the practical things – that's what I'm good at. I suppose I could have given her more space, but I didn't know what to do. There weren't any rules, and I was only young, too.

Caro: Wednesday morning, Ferry Cottage

The hospital has sent me lots of pieces of paper and a list of what to pack. I'm allowed to take my wedding ring, but no photos. I would have liked to have had a photo of Mark with me, the one outside the cottage the day we first saw it. Nix must have taken it.

Mark and I have always been at our newly-wed best. I've always assumed we would have lasted the course, but who knows? I can't imagine how our lives would be now; I can't imagine the look of a Mark who's grown older.

Not that I'm particularly old. Not old enough for all this.

I would have liked to have had a photo of Mark with me. It upsets me that I can't really remember the reality of him now.

Nix: Thursday morning, Plymouth Express.

I should be working on plans for a client, but I'm starting to get a headache. Caro said it was a shame that I put all my artistic talent into straight lines and angles.

I wonder if her hair is still that lovely golden blonde? She was so pretty when she was little. I bet she hasn't gone grey like me.

I rang the hospital before I got on the train. I was passed around from pillar to post, but eventually I found the right department. They said that Caro was going into surgery this morning, and that someone would talk to me when I got to the hospital.

Always the thought, niggling away: I could have done more to help her before this.

Caro: Wednesday morning, Ferry Cottage
The taxi's here. Jim's driving. I wish it was someone I didn't know; sometimes I don't feel I can make conversation.

Keys.
Money.
Wedding ring.

My bag. Just a few things. Sorry, Jim, I can't quite manage... would you mind?

No, nothing serious. No, really, I'm fine. Thank you for your concern. Just a bit of a problem with headaches. No, I'm not sure yet when I'll need picking up.

Not proper laughing, though. Nervous laughing.

I've left a list on the kitchen table for when it's all over, just in case I can't remember.

Unpack bag
Rosie > spare keys
Phone Nix again?

Clues. Lifelines.

As well as a list, I've left Nix's phone number, in case someone needs to call her, and a separate letter for her, just in case.

Nix: Thursday afternoon, Plymouth Express.

Lots of people are getting off at Exeter. There's nothing stopping me doing the same. Caro probably phoned me on a whim, without thinking, and I've taken emergency leave from work and dashed down to Cornwall like a mad woman. I could get off the train here, get the next one home. What am I going to say to her anyway?

Except. Except I didn't get a good feeling from the woman at the hospital when I rang earlier. I always like to look on the bright side, but still, it unnerved me.

I don't think Caro and I ever had a big argument or anything like that. It was more of a loosening, an unpicking of threads. It's easier sometimes, to be around in a crisis; the difficult bit is negotiating the progress of the long haul. A couple of months after Mark's accident, I was down at Ferry Cottage for the weekend. Caro had been looking through Mark's things and she'd found a poster of Jimi Hendrix, of all people, that Mark had had on the wall of his student digs. Well past his sell-by date, even then. I got the bin bags so we could start throwing some stuff away. I threw away the poster, thinking that would be an uncomplicated place to start.

Caro accused me of trying to tidy Mark away. She said I'd been the same when Dad died.

I don't think I was, but somebody has to do the difficult things.

That day was the nearest we came to an argument. I'm sure she said she didn't want to see me again. I didn't consciously stop going to Ferry Cottage, but I went down less and less. Caro just didn't want to be helped. And then later, I was too busy, and time just went by, the way time does.

45

And I was, *really* busy. Especially after Tim left, when I was on my own with the boys. I didn't see that one coming. I thought we were fine; it never even entered my head. I might have taken it better if I'd had some warning, but I just had to get on and make the best of it.

If Mark had lived, would he and Caro still be together? They were so happy the first time they saw Ferry Cottage; they didn't seem to see the old Coke cans caught in the matted reeds by the broken jetty, or smell the stagnant water at low tide.

I hope the hospital smells of antiseptic. I don't trust hospitals that don't smell clean.

Tidy up. Guardian, wine gums, flask on the table. Holdall ready; just a few things packed, just in case.

What on earth am I going to say to her after all these years?

Caro: Wednesday morning, Ferry Cottage
I can't get used to seeing the estate agent's sign outside.

Thanks Jim. Yes, I'm up for sale. Or rather the cottage is. You're right, it'll be a wrench. A terrible wrench. But you know how it is… and it needs so much work still…

I wonder whether Nix got my message. I know she'll come, even after all this time. I won't push her away again. She'll be my lifeline.

The razor-sharp sunrise has softened into a pale orange that's fading to blue almost as I watch it. When I get home, I'll collect wild garlic for soup, and I'll paint the hedgerows in their rainbow greens.

I've left a list on the kitchen table, and a letter, just in case.

HEARTBEAT
March 1967

When their village hit the headlines, and the men found their way to the Ship, drawn to the pub even if they weren't normally drinkers, the women had Roberto's hair salon for their news. In the salon, they were rushed off their feet at the best of times, but now their regulars were popping in every five minutes, whether they had an appointment or not. *What's the date of my next perm? And while I'm here... I see they've brought the Air Force in.* Customers who'd given up their appointment slots and blue rinses over the past couple of years, in favour of the unisex salons in town, were flocking back. It wasn't the same as coming here, they said. *If you could just squeeze me in for a shampoo and set?* Nothing happened very often, so when it did, no-one wanted to miss a thing.

The girls never got their hour's break at lunchtime, and didn't really expect to, not a full hour. 'But if I don't get a break,' said Grace, 'I'm off. *Comprendo?*' She unearthed an enamel sign from the bottom of the airing cupboard – CLOSED FOR LUNCH – a bit rusty around the edges, but to the point. She replaced the string and handed it to Robert. 'Or else,' she said.

Robert locked the salon door, put the sign up, and went to fetch his telly down from his flat so that they could watch the lunchtime news. Grace and Stella perched on stools in the small back storeroom. Stella unwrapped her sandwiches, carefully refolding the greaseproof paper. 'Egg and salad cream. You?' Grace turned up her nose and put her own fish paste sandwiches to one side.

'Can one of you give me a hand?' The sound of a door

slamming, and muffled swearing came from the stairwell.

'I'm in the lav!' Grace shouted back and Stella giggled and choked on her lunch.

Grace took her new afghan coat from the hook behind the door. She put it on over her mauve tabard, flicking her straight, centre-parted hair out from the fur around the neckline.

'Do you have to?' said Stella. 'That thing stinks… dead fox.'

'You're just jealous.' Grace carefully traced the embroidery down the front panels. 'Everyone's wearing them in London.'

'Like who?'

'John Lennon,' said Grace. Stella pulled a face. 'Twiggy.'

'She's got no sense of smell, then,' said Stella. 'Please. Hang it out in the yard. It's not like it's cold in here.'

Grace wasn't going to admit it, but she was hot as hell, what with all the heat from the driers in the two main rooms of the salon, plus the hot water boiler going flat out all day. But she wasn't going to let that stop her wearing the coat whenever she could. She'd bought it with her first month's proper wages after she got promoted from trainee. It was an investment in her future. It was a shame about the smell. The ones imported from India didn't smell, apparently, but she couldn't afford a genuine one.

'Thank you so much for your help, ladies,' said Robert as he squashed sideways through the door with the TV. He untangled the lead and struggled behind the shelves to reach a socket.

'Are you alright?' Stella said to Grace. 'You look…'

Grace tore off her coat and ran towards the toilet, hand over her mouth. The sickness came suddenly and violently, and she tried to be quiet, not to retch.

She swilled out her mouth and splashed cold water over her face. She knew she looked like death on legs so put on her brightest smile and breezed back in the room, avoiding Stella's eye.

'Is it catching?' said Robert.

'Fish paste.' Grace swallowed hard and shivered, cold now despite the heat in the room. She put her coat round her shoulders and pushed Robert off her stool. 'Move over,' she said. 'It'll be on soon.'

There was a distant boom, followed by another and another, and for a moment Grace thought the noise was coming from the screen. But it was real life.

'They're bombing again,' Stella said. 'They said they would.'

Grace didn't regard her position at Roberto's as a long-term prospect, more of a stepping stone to bigger, brighter things. In London, hairdressers were part of a glamorous world, alongside pop stars, fashion designers and photographers, she'd seen it in magazines. On her bedroom wall, she sellotaped a poster of a London bus in Carnaby Street, and a picture of Mary Quant that she cut out of the Daily Mirror. Grace had dreams. The afghan coat was her first step towards achieving them.

Starting as a Saturday girl, she traded time at the beach for money of her own, and the first chance to save up some money for her escape fund. She enjoyed the work. Washing hair (*What shampoo would you like? Ordinary or dandruff?*), and tying the hairnets, placing pink foam circles over the ladies' ears to stop them burning under the driers. Offering magazines, making tea. She listened to what the women said about men. She learned a lot, but she should have listened more carefully.

In the storeroom, they waited for the TV to warm up. They still had five minutes before the start of the programme. Until the BBC sent a reporter down especially from London, nobody in the village had been particularly concerned. The consensus in Roberto's was that it would all sort it itself out in due course. And if the boats couldn't get out for a few days – well, there was always work long overdue fixing engines, nets and tackle. But reports of the oil spill shifted up the running

49

order until it became the lead story, and suddenly there were people everywhere, all round the village. Reporters, experts, students, hippy-types and plain old nosey parkers, offering help, asking questions, and generally getting in the way.

Robert twiddled the aerial until the horizontal hold stopped looping. Grace, still feeling queasy, tried to take deep breaths without being obvious, then the theme tune started, then the panning opening shot –

'That's your mum's!' Stella squealed, and dug her elbow into Grace's side. And there it was for the whole world to see. The terrace of cottages, her mum's at the very end nearest the harbour, neat and trim, and behind, the long stone shed that had been her dad's territory while he was alive. The camera passed over the whitewashed cottage and lingered on the rusty roof of the shed, rotten through in places, easily fixed but steadfastly unfixed; the window glass intact, but cross-webbed and dark, the frames softened by moss and ferns; and outside the shed, a coil of rope rotting into the grass, and a pile of shredded nets and lobster pots woven together by bramble. Grace could imagine the other fishermen watching this, shaking their heads at the clear evidence of unforgiveable waste. They could have had use of the net loft and all that gear, all perfectly usable, except for the fact that Marissa, Grace's mother, was letting it all go to rack and ruin. The shot panned back to the cottage, neat as a pin, then round, past the old mine stacks, and out to sea, where they could see the oil like a shadow of a storm, and the listing tanker, and then a white spume as the first salvo of bombs hit the water.

'That was definitely your mum's,' said Robert and they peered at the fuzzy square of their little village by the sea like it was foreign land they'd never seen before, and they watched until the picture snowed over. Robert turned the aerial and then Stan from the Ship appeared on the screen suddenly, alarmingly, dressed in a suit and tie like he was off to a funeral, telling the camera about the holidaymakers and how they'd lose their summer trade unless something got done, and pronto.

There was something about seeing it all unfold on the news that changed how they felt. They knew that outside the harbour and all along the coast, crude oil was arriving in thick, slow moving blankets, and sticking and covering everything in its path. The smell of oil and detergent everywhere was enough to make you gag. They all knew about the seabirds lying in black, thick oil. But there was something about seeing it all compressed onto a 16 x 12-inch screen and hearing it described by a BBC reporter in a posh, serious voice that made it so much more real.

They were showing the earlier bombing of the oil slick on the news, and they could hear bombing now, in real life. 'It's like the war,' said Robert, and Stella rolled her eyes and yawned. Grace couldn't see how bombing the oil would help but they were running out of ideas. They'd tried to scoop up the oil. Some of it got dumped in the old quarries. Then detergent; then napalm; then millions of free-floating, uncatchable drops.

The salon doorbell rang. Robert said to Grace, 'Better open up.'

'It's still our lunch hour, officially.' She felt the need to establish the point but went out anyway. Stella followed her.

'You sure you're alright?' Stella caught hold of her wrist and whispered, 'I know someone who can help.'

Grace pulled away, took down the closed sign and opened the door. Instead of one of their regulars, there was a woman in her thirties, dressed like she'd come off the boats – oilskins and yellow boots, red wind-burnt cheeks, dark curly hair scraped back into a ponytail. Grace stood at the door, protecting the clean lino.

'I won't come in,' said the woman.

'We haven't got anything at the moment,' Grace said. 'We're fully booked. But I can fetch the book. Next week, we might be able to fit you in.' She looked at the woman's hair, wiry, with split ends, and made a mental note to block out a double slot. The woman had a fish crate by her feet, covered in a piece of sacking. She bent down and lifted the corner to show Grace what she had.

'We thought... well I thought, I know it's an imposition but...' the woman straightened up and looked at her. 'I hate asking. But I have to do something.'

Robert said no, but Grace stood her ground, threatening to leave and take Stella with her. Appointments were cancelled. They got out all their towels, even the old ones they used for perms and colours that were stained with hair dye and patchy with bleach.

Although she'd been brought up just a stone's throw from the sea, Grace had never learned the names of the seabirds, or how to differentiate one bird from another. If she had to refer to them at all, she called them gulls, generically, thinking that was good enough. Someone told her that most of the birds they were bringing in were either guillemots or razorbills, but there were others, just a mass of feathers and oil. Blistered and singed, froth bubbling around their beaks where they'd been preening and preening to try to clean themselves, and swallowing oil and detergent in the process.

When it came to picking up the first bird, Grace had a moment when she didn't think she could. She retched emptily into the basin. The bird was wrapped up in a piece of black, oil-soaked cloth, its legs struggling feebly for some kind of purchase, its head hanging as if it were broken, but eyes wild and alive. She wanted to run out of the salon, out of the village, to somewhere this wasn't happening. Stella, a farmer's daughter, was already stuck in. 'And we thought your coat stank,' she said. Grace swallowed hard and forced herself to pick up the bird and take it to one of the back basins, and unwrap it, and start the process of trying to break down the oil with shampoo and hot water.

People came to help, bringing towels, sheets, whatever they could find. They soon learned that a bucket system worked best, passing the birds from basin to basin. They put a crate on the floor for the birds that died in the process. The smell was like hell on earth, and the birds were covered in oil, and they were covered too, and the salon, and Robert started talking about compensation until the girls told him to shut up.

Marissa had no comprehension of why Grace would try to save a wild creature which would die eventually, if not this way, then another. Throughout all the fuss and furore, she continued her daily fight against the elements, against sand and salt, moss and damp, to keep their cottage as pristine as any in the county, despite the fact that it almost sat in the sea. Once, she'd had dreams, just like her daughter. She thought she'd marry a man from the city, but a fisherman caught her, and Marissa had been overwhelmed by their watery romance. She blamed herself for not putting up more of a struggle. Grace had been soon-born. The longer she was married, the more Marissa's skin dried out and cracked in the air, and the heavier her movements became. She was still a young woman, but the land had aged her. Her husband, dead three years, offered love at first, but no understanding. The other fishermen said that Marissa brought bad luck.

Inside the cottage, the key to the shed hung on a nail behind the pantry door. Not to be touched, but it was there for the taking. Inside the shed were Grace's dad's clothes, locked away since the day he died. Not much. Oilskins, sou'westers, boots and socks. Thick woollen jumpers. Everything was dumped in a pile on the earth floor. It stank like a sea creature's carcass. Grace stole the key and took her dad's old overalls into the salon.

Grace and the others soon learned that some birds were so frightened and sick that it wasn't worth trying to save them. Grace learned to distinguish one bird from another: herring gulls from black-backed gulls, the guillemots from razorbills. She often carried on working even after Robert had gone up to his flat, and Stella and the volunteers had all gone home, dead on their feet, backs aching, hands raw, eyes raw. Grace sang as she worked. It seemed to soothe the birds and quieten her own worries. She cradled the birds, and sang to them, feeling their tiny hearts beating almost out of their bodies.

Stella said, 'Are you sure you should be doing this?'

Grace pretended not to know what she was talking about, and laughed and said 'Of course, what about you?'

They tried to stop every lunchtime, just for half an hour, for a quick sandwich and a cup of tea. Robert's telly was still in the storeroom and they watched the news telling their story.

The BBC arrived one morning to interview them. Robert told them that Grace had worked the hardest and so they asked her to tell them what it was like. She told them how it was to cradle those birds in her hands, and feel their heartbeats racing, and how it felt when she couldn't save them. The words didn't come out right, but she tried to explain as best she could.

Marissa watched the TV. She saw Grace wearing her father's overalls, stolen from the shed and washed in secret. She saw what was clear for everyone to see: the curved belly under the overalls, the extra weight carried around the hips, the gap between buttons, the slight strain on the fabric. She did not ask. She waited to be told.

People came who knew how to care properly for the birds. The bombing stopped and the village started to fade from the headlines. Their story had been told to the world and now it was wrapped up and finished, as far as the reporters were concerned.

The day the last Outside Broadcast van left the village, and all the reporters had checked out of the Ship, Grace stole the shed key again and folded her dad's overalls, washed but oil-stained, and placed them carefully on a shelf. Then she went up to her room. Her dad had battened it out and plastered it years ago, so she had proper flat walls, not like the rough stone everywhere else. He'd fitted an electric heater, but still the windows froze on the inside in winter, and since he'd died, she wasn't allowed to use the heater. Her mother didn't feel the cold, and they couldn't afford it anyway. There was carpet downstairs, covering the slates, impractical but one of her mother's insistences: 'We are NOT animals'. Grace and her dad were always joined by a smile, one to the other across the kitchen table, at these commandments. Marissa was excluded, never part of the team.

Grace told her saved-up story to her mother. Marissa had carefully stored up her anger while she waited for this telling. Grace would be tied here too; this was the cycle, repeating, repeating, repeating as tides. There was fury from both of them. Not at the baby, but at Grace's refusal to name the father, let alone accept him as husband.

Her mother knew that clothes held power, even old clothes, even the clothes of the drowned and the lost. In the storm of her anger, she tried to take Grace's precious coat from her. It fell into the fire in the struggle, but Grace saved it. The burn on Grace's forearm faded away quickly; the burn on the sleeve of her coat was like a brand, reminding her of her homestead.

Grace moved out, and the following day, her mother started wallpapering her room with Anaglypta, and painting it white, opening the windows wide to get rid of the smell of that coat. The poster of Carnaby Street and the picture of Mary Quant went straight in the bin, along with the other things that Grace couldn't carry.

The fishermen's wives and the other neighbours had another reason to be angry at the widow. *What about the girl's things? She's got a room above the salon, best thing for her. No, he's not... just being a friend. That woman's not fit to call herself a mother.*

But Grace knew her mother couldn't help herself. Trapped too long out of her element, this was what she had become.

Robert let Grace have the spare room in the flat, just to see her over until she got herself sorted. When the baby was born, Grace inhaled the smell of her, searching for the slightest tang of the sea. She inspected her tiny perfect fingers and toes for any sign of the joining of skin, any hint of a legacy passing down the maternal line. She was going to call her Mary, after Mary Quant, but decided instead on Joan, after Joan Baez. Grace knew the power of names. Joan would grow up fearless and brave. They ended up staying in the flat for longer than they ever expected. The smell of the afghan coat faded. Grace slept with it on top of her bed.

Whenever one of her regulars mentioned her mother, hoping for Grace to bad-mouth her or give them some sort of inside scoop, she just carried on putting in curlers, or sectioning hair, or dabbing on dye, or whatever she was doing. More than anyone, Grace understood that her mother hadn't been born to this life. She'd thought she'd wanted the land, but like selkies everywhere, she always longed for the other place. Grace knew from the way Marissa watched the seals that she felt the call of the sea that she could never return to, and felt that torment every day of her life.

From the attic window in the flat above the salon, Grace could see the sea rippling across the sky. The cries of the gulls circled around her. Sometimes she dreamed of darting through water like a seal, sleek and agile, and sometimes she dreamed of beating hearts and beating wings. The smell of oil faded but never disappeared completely from the beach, where the polluted sand was bulldozed and buried, to be stirred to the surface after every storm.

NOAH
July 15th 2022

Chloe Bolitho's got a boyfriend, or at least it looks like things might be heading that way. Every time she happens to be sitting on her favourite bench on the harbour wall, it seems that he's walking past with his scraggy terrier. He nods sometimes. They've progressed to the stage where he might stop and say 'Hi', and they'll both look out to sea for a bit before he says, 'Bye then,' and leaves.

She knows where he lives, or to be precise, she knows where his family stay when they come down for the holidays. His mum and dad have got one of the 1950s chalet bungalows on the no-through-road that runs behind and above the harbour. Extended up and out, like all the bungalows, its balconies are Juliet, the garden decked, the riviera palm uplit in the evenings. A crab pot squats by the front door. Rope instead of a handrail hugs the front steps and there are hooks for wetsuits and a tap by the back door. Like all the other front-row houses, it's Farrow-and-Balled in unlikely sounding maritime shades, dressed up in faux New England clam-chowder chic.

Chloe Bolitho notices details like these. She doesn't make a big thing of it, but she wants to be a poet and practises seeing everyday things in new and interesting ways. She keeps a journal and highlights the thoughts and phrases that she's particularly proud of. What started as way of spilling the pain of her dad and the pain of herself onto a plain white surface, has become something more. It was her secret but now she's more open and she enjoys the whole action of taking out her notebook and writing in public. One day she hopes someone will stop beside her and ask her what she's doing.

Chloe lives with her mum on the new estate on the edge of town, where the houses are banged up together and people are always arguing about parking spaces. She'd be able to see his house above the harbour if she stood on the seat of the toilet upstairs and stuck her head out of the window.

She knows his name is Ross, she heard his mother talking to him in the shop one day. She thinks he might be artistic, or he could be just thin and sickly looking, she can't quite make up her mind. If she were being brutally honest, she would have to admit that he is spotty, but at least you can trust a boy with spots. This thought makes her laugh, and she writes it in her journal. It's material, something she might be able to use one day.

He looks like he'd break easily, or he would really mark if you scratched him accidentally. His skin is almost see-through across the bridge of his nose and the tops of his cheeks. He looks like he's never played rugby, ridden a jet-ski, done the Ten Tors, gone mackerel fishing or got sick on Home Farm cider, all of which are plus points to Chloe. She recognises a fellow cornflake-box kid, and wonders whether he still reads the backs of cereal packets at breakfast like she does, and whether he was always being told off for having his nose in a book instead of playing outside or doing something useful. He definitely looks like he needs looking after.

Half-way through July, and it's a day of blue skies and puffy white clouds that look like they belong in a painting. The tide is on its way out and the first trip-round-the-bay boats, and trawlers, and small yachts, are leaving the harbour, sending white-capped wave-arrows out behind them. Chloe isn't starting at the caravan site until ten, so she's sitting on her bench trying to write the view in front of her, except its picture-postcard perfectness becomes tired and clichéd as soon as she tries to put it down on paper.

Ross arrives, and in a departure from their normal routine, he sits down at the far end of her bench, distanced, but without a doubt inside her personal space. Released from its lead, the dog shoots down to the exposed margin of wet sand, tail helicoptering like it's trying to take flight, and starts digging its way to Australia, shooting seaweed high into the air. Ross tells her all about the dog. How it was a rescue dog and how timid it had been, and Chloe decides to give him the benefit of the doubt and puts his excessive dog-love down to nerves. Chloe Bolitho knows she can be off-putting sometimes.

'What's its name?'

'Dog,' he says.

He asks her name, and she hesitates for a micro-moment. This would be a good chance to try out one of the new names she's been considering to better reflect her poet persona, but she gives him a straightforward 'Chloe,' instead.

'Yours?' she asks, even though she knows.

'Noah.'

'Your mum calls you Ross.'

'Ross is my real name. Fucking Poldark,' he sighs and looks tragic.

'Yeah,' Chloe says, weirdly loud and over-emphatic. 'Fucking Poldark.'

'It was OK, you know, while I was growing up and no-one made the connection. But then it was all over the TV and...'

She nods. She feels that they've made a breakthrough.

His parents have got a thing about Cornwall, he tells her, as if she couldn't have guessed. They tell everyone that Kernow is their spiritual home. His sister is called Demelza, but she refuses to answer to it.

'Why Noah?' She's interested in the process of renaming yourself. 'How did you decide?'

'I don't know. It just settled.'

She stops herself saying – 'And you called the dog 'Dog'? Is that really the best you could come up with?'

Her shifts get all tangled up at the caravan park, and they ask her to help out at the Spar, so she doesn't see him for a few days. When she does get the chance to get down to the harbour, she makes an effort. It's a stonking hot morning. Chloe is wearing a ditsy print dress from Oxfam and look-alike DMs but knows she's not quite pulling it off, achieving quirky, but in just the wrong kind of way, and she's worried she looks like she's trying too hard. Chloe Bolitho doesn't know how pretty she is. Her dad used to tell her she was a stunner, but he was her dad, and that was his job.

From her bench, she can see Noah coming down the bank from the road to the harbour wall. She engrosses herself in her journal, reading the same sentence over and over. He arrives. He sits down. On the bench. Quite close. He lets Dog off its lead. Chloe can barely breathe.

'Hi,' he says. He's dressed head to toe in Superdry. It looks like a present from his mum and dad when they should really have just given him the money.

'Nice tee-shirt,' she says.

'My mum. Birthday. She thought it would help me fit in down here.'

'Yeah, like we're all so designer,' Chloe says.

It turns out that Dog is more whippet than terrier and can travel faster than the speed of light, and suddenly it has bulleted back from the beach.

'Jesus!' Chloe screams. 'Get that fucking dog off my fucking leg!'

Dog is all wild eyes and determined concentration.

Noah tries to pull the dog off her leg. 'Sorry. Sorry!'

'Does it even know how ugly it is?'

'Harsh,' he says.

'Get it seen to at the vets. It's disgusting.'

Noah clips the lead back on Dog and they set off. Dog looks back to her, and she thinks, bastard dog would wink if it could. Its whiskers remind her of something her dad used to watch on TV when he was stuck in bed. *Steptoe.*

Who needs a boyfriend anyway?

He turns up again the next day. She's engrossed in striking matches and flicking them over the harbour wall and doesn't see him coming.

'Sorry about...' he says.

She shrugs and strikes another match.

'Do you smoke?' he asks.

'No. Where's Dog?'

'At home.' He sits down but doesn't extend his arm along the back of the bench or make any sort of move into her personal space.

'You're always here,' he says, and it's a question, the loaded one, although he's not to know that. What should she tell him? Chloe Bolitho wants to be a poet, and so she knows about finding a narrative, about selection and editing. She knows that there are multiple stories and multiple versions of the truth. She knows about unreliable narrators.

She decides – for now – to keep it simple and just tell him about her dad. She hits him with her killer phrase.

'By the way, you're sitting on my dad.'

She watches the confusion in his face. Then he reads the inscription: *Tom Bolitho 1981 - 2021.*

'Your dad?'

She nods.

'Last year?'

She nods.

'I'm sorry.'

'Why? It's not your fault.' How many times has she said

that to people over the past year?

'That's awful,' he says.

Chloe says it's OK, it's all fine, although it really, really, really is not.

There were other things she could have said to Noah, but telling him about her dad was the most obvious line to take. She has this idea that every time she sits on this bench and leans back against the gold lettering, the words 'Forever in Our Hearts' transfer themselves to her, like she's growing a second layer of skin, built up of impressions of these words.

Forever in our hearts. He loved this view.

'What do you do when you're not sitting here?' he says.

She doesn't go round telling people that she wants to be a poet. She's not stupid.

'I've got jobs – cleaning, bar work…'

'Right,' he says, and she thinks, *What? Not good enough for you, city boy?*

'Actually, I want to be a poet,' she says. 'Yeah. I'm going to be a poet.'

'Cool. Can I hear some of your stuff?'

And it's just as simple and straightforward as that. She's going to be a poet. She just needs to open her mouth and let the words flow.

'You?' she asks.

'Nuclear physicist.'

'Oh.' She tries to keep the disappointment out of her voice. But thinks, optimistically, that you can probably still be artistic even if you're a scientist.

'Quark is an amazing word,' she says. 'Strangeness and charm.'

'If you say so.' Noah looks confused.

Chloe Bolitho knows that Noah isn't going to be a boyfriend, but she knows that he is solid friend material. She avoids her mates from school, back from Uni. They haven't got anything

63

in common anymore, and pretending they have is just awkward and embarrassing for them all.

'I'm going down the beach tonight. Do you want to come?' she says. 'You don't have to. But if you like. I'll make a fire. There won't be anyone else. I don't mean... not like ...'

'Mum's got marshmallows at home.'

'OK. That's good. Marshmallows are good. Seven? Or whenever...?'

'OK.'

'Don't bring Dog.'

She gets to the beach early, disturbing yellow-footed egrets and a flurry of oystercatchers that lift and settle further down the beach. She collects silver-dry driftwood from the bottom of the cliffs above the high-tide mark, filling a bag with plastic detritus as she goes. Some of it is identifiable – water bottles, screw tops, flip-flops, fishing line, baler wrap. Most of it is already degrading into faded, edge-softened rectangles and squares. Some of the plastic particles are so small that she can't separate them out, and she wonders if one day all the sand here will be completely replaced by ice-cream shades of pink and turquoise and green. There's been another small collapse along the cliff; the engine house has been taken another few metres closer to the sea. The new-fallen soil is raw and empty as if a digger's been through it and removed all traces of grass and scrub. The freshly exposed cliff face is dotted with random circles where rabbit tunnels have fallen away; they open out now onto a sheer drop.

Chloe has brought a large box of matches and BBQ lighter fluid. She doesn't want the embarrassment of not being able to light a bonfire on the beach; she's a local after all. They used to have bonfires down here all the time, she and her mates from school, drinking, smoking, messing around. But fire can be fickle, she knows.

After the baby was lost, Chloe had come down to the beach and made a bonfire. She knew she had to give the baby a name. She chose Alice. Chloe is the only person who knows this name, so she has all the magic of it to herself. There's no memorial bench, no plaque, no inscription. She has nothing to show, nothing to share. Just a name, but Chloe knows that naming is important.

She picks up a stone, round and smooth, skims it. Five perfect skips, her lucky number, and she says out loud five things she wants to happen. Not wild wishes, just five perfectly possible future things.

The fire smoulders slowly, then takes, spitting as it flares. She wonders if Noah will turn up. Part of her hopes he doesn't, so she can sit alone with her own thoughts, making up rhymes and rhythms in her head that dance with the rhymes and the rhythms of the fire and the sea. But the part of her that's ready for good, possible, future things, is looking forward to Noah arriving. She just wants to be normal, have a laugh, muck around without all the stuff she's already accumulated in her life, with someone who doesn't know her, so she can start again with a clean slate and be whoever she wants to be.

Noah is walking along the wall towards the headland. Dog is pulling him on; he tried to leave him behind, but his mum insisted. He hopes that Chloe won't shout at him.

Chloe watches his awkward and gawky progress over the rocks towards her. Then she sees he's got Dog with him, and that he's carrying a guitar.

Her mum's always going on about how Chloe needs a boyfriend, someone nice and steady who'll make her laugh, but it's not going to be a guitar-strumming city-boy with spots and a dog that's the reincarnation of a dirty old man from the telly. But Chloe is really glad he's come. He's good friend material, and she can tell her mum they're going out together, that will keep her quiet on the subject.

Chloe Bolitho wants someone to hear her. She thinks she can be a poet because of the sadness, and the pain and the guilt that overwhelm her sometimes, completely and utterly in a way that she struggles to name or describe. She thinks about perfectly possible future things that might happen; she hopes it might be possible to make poems out of those things too.

Bilateral Breathing
April 2022

You feel slow as a snail as you cycle up the last steep hill between school and home, the dead weight of your rucksack full of books pulling on your shoulders. Mind over matter is the key. You divert yourself by thinking about what you'd be doing if you were at after-school practice at the swimming pool where you used to live; putting in laps, practicing tumble turns and bilateral breathing, turning your head to one side then the other, finding a rhythm. You forget about cycling. You imagine gliding like a seal through water and you visualise perfecting your stroke and form. It works. You reach the top of the hill without being aware of the effort of the climb. You exhale/inhale deeply, filling your lungs, and prop your bike against the field gate. The lambs are hunkered down in the shelter of the hedges out of the firing line of the bitter north-easterly. You can just about see the sea from here, a triangle caught between two hills; you probably wouldn't even realise it was sea unless you knew it was there. It's another four miles before you reach home, but it's mostly downhill with a couple of gentle rises. You could ring for a lift now that you've got a signal but it's good exercise and you wouldn't ask anyway.

You don't share your parents' enthusiasm for your new life in the country and you'd never admit to liking anything about it, on principle. But there are some good things. The lambs are one of your secret sources of joy; you've stopped here on the way back from school ever since they were tiny and shaky on their legs. The lambs are chunky now, not really lambs anymore, but on sunny afternoons they still race from one end of the field to the other, jumping, cartoon-startled, with all four hooves off the ground at once, the absolute definition of frolicking. But today, the wind is so fierce, and the ewes and their lambs are sitting it out, having a collective duvet day.

You've been living for six months in the dream cottage that your parents have bought in the middle of nowhere. It's not even near the sea, because your parent's couldn't afford that kind of dream cottage, so you can't even go swimming. You go to the small local school and do small local things and you should be so much happier. And you know you're ungrateful, so you try to be nice but that seems completely impossible sometimes. This has been a coming home for your mum; she was brought up nearby in all this green and pleasantness. Your auntie and cousin Chloe live down on the coast, but you're stuck up on the edge of the moors, surrounded by abandoned copper mines and desolation, the sea barely visible from the tops of the tors.

You hear a car coming; its engine revs as it takes the steep corner by the track that leads to the farm next door. It will be someone you know because no-one comes down these lanes unless they live around here. Your split-second thought, *have I got time to hide?* But you know you won't be able to get your bike behind the hedge in time. Whoever it is, they'll stop and talk to you. Why does everyone always want to chat? Everyone gossiping, asking, noseying around.

The car stops beside you, a black Mitsubishi 4WD. You know who that is.

'Hi Emma, you OK? Want a lift?'

'I've got my bike.'

'That's alright. Stick it in the back and hop in.'

I'm not a rabbit, you want to say, but you know how childish it sounds so you don't say anything. You don't want to get into the Mitsubishi, but he's already out of the car and picking up your bike.

68

Alan is a feed merchant, although you're not sure what that is. He went to school with your mum, but he looks younger than she does, perhaps because he's so outdoorsy and hearty, like meat pie and gravy.

'Don't worry about the mud,' he says, and you say OK, and you smile inside because he's obviously worried about your muddy trainers or he wouldn't have said it. There are long strands of grass caught in the wing mirrors and around the wheels of the Mitsubishi, but it's really clean inside and a traffic light pine air freshener hangs from the mirror so the car smells of school toilets and chicken pellets all mixed-up together. You breathe shallowly, barely moving your chest, trying not to taste the air molecules that are trapped between you and him.

You don't care about his car, but you don't want to give him the satisfaction of having to clean up after you. You can imagine him down the pub later, telling them all that he'd given you a lift. Because that's the level of conversation around here. All the sly looks, and the under-talk. 'Oh, he gave Jenny's daughter a lift, eh?' Because everyone knows about him and your mum, they just pretend not to.

So, you decide to keep your feet off the floor, then there'll be no mud. You tighten your abdominals, squeeze your glutes, engage your core. This is no problem for you; you've had years of swim training, doing drills and practicing form, and strength work and endurance sessions, so this is a breeze. You hover your feet just over the passenger mat, so he won't notice what you're doing.

'How's school?'

You don't answer. Who does he think he is, your dad or something?

A strong core, it's the key to everything, that's what your dad says. He's an Iron Man, always training; it takes hours of effort every week just to maintain his baseline fitness level, and

69

ramping up before a competition is more like a full-time job. Even if you'd rung for a lift from the top of the hill, he probably wouldn't be available, he'd be running along the coast path, or kayaking the estuary or cycling some ridiculous distance on his super-light, super-expensive titanium-framed bike, or running up and down the hills at the back of the house in tight black Lycra. In the lead up to an event, you rarely see him. His strongest discipline is cycling, and he wants you to take it up seriously. He's says you've got talent, could make a go of it, if you put in some work. He says he'll make a programme for you, and perhaps you can ride out together sometimes.

Your mum is encouraging, she'd like you and your father to spend more time together. Neither of your parents seem to want to take you the long drive to the pool, and swimming in the sea is much too dangerous, they say, although your dad goes in to keep up his tri-training. If you were being really unreasonable, you'd say that they were deliberately stopping you doing the one thing you love doing.

You slide your hand under your thighs, palms to the plush, knuckles pressed into your legs. Nearly there. Hold your feet up. No gain without pain, your dad's favourite phrase. Tough it out. Mind over matter.

'How's your mum getting on? I haven't seen her for a while.'

You don't answer. Alan was one of the first people your mum and dad invited over for dinner when you moved down here. He's divorced. You know he goes go to Friday film night in the Church Hall, like your mum does, and sits on the fête committee that your mum had just joined. Your dad doesn't do 'community' things. When he's at home, he's too busy freelancing, whatever that means, and the rest of the time he's out training or away competing.

Alan drives too fast, everyone does around here. No-one seems to notice that the lanes are narrow, or care that there might be a person on a bike, or an animal, around one of the sharp bends. Even on the quiet lanes that you cycle on the way to and from school, the road kill is gross. Rabbits, squirrels, frogs, pheasants; you're not sure if you're supposed to move dead things into the hedgerows or leave them to be eaten by buzzards and crows.

Your abs are starting to pulse with the effort of holding your feet off the floor.

'Your mum says you're going to have a go at competitive cycling,' Alan says. 'You're going to need something better than that old bone shaker.'

'That's my dad's idea,' you say. 'I'm a swimmer.'

'Really?'

'Didn't Mum tell you? I swam for the County where we used to live.'

'Well done you! But we don't really go in for swimming round here. Your mum knows. Get her to tell you about the selkie folk.'

You feel like you've been dropped into some cheesy old film, where the locals deliver cryptic utterances and chew bits of grass, and the pub sign creaks in the wind, and the stranger doesn't listen to all the dire warnings.

Alan's laughing, hitting the steering wheel in his mirth. 'The look on your face! Selkie folk!'

You feel red heat creeping up your neck across your cheeks through your hair, and you stare fixedly out of the car window at the boring, the boring, the boring outside, and the more you wish it away, the hotter you feel.

He puts on a yokel accent, 'Beware the selkie creatures of the sea.'

He turns the pick-up into your lane.

'You're screwing my mum, aren't you?' you say. 'You can let me out here if you want.'

He opens his mouth, closes it, repeats, like a goldfish. You know it's probably not even true. It's just a story you've made that might fit all the facts. But it's said now, and you don't know how to unsay it.

His face is red and blotchy. He stops the car, and you open the door and manage to swing round without letting your feet touch the mat. He doesn't try to follow you. Your skanky old bike is still in the back of his pick-up, but you just want to get away as quickly as possible, and hide, and not have to explain this to anyone.

If you were at home, your real home, you'd be at swimming club now, getting your laps in, practicing tumble turns and bilateral breathing. You'd be gliding like a seal through water, efficient, strong, confident, in your element.

Your mum's just shut the oven door. She's wearing a flowery apron and has flour on her cheek like a soldier stripe. You know you won't be able to get upstairs without being interrogated about your day. You've run up the lane from Alan's car, and you pretend to be more out of breath than you are, so you don't have to answer her questions.

'How was school? What did you do? Do you want some cake? I've made lemon drizzle.'

You shake your head.

'Where's your bike?'

'In the back of Alan's pick-up.'

'He gave you a lift? Why didn't you ask him in for a cup of tea? Dinner's at half six!' she shouts at your back.

You lie on your bed. You should start your maths homework, but you do nothing at all. You wait for the sound of a siren, or a flashing light, or someone knocking on the door, but nothing happens. Nothing at all.

Downstairs, you hear your mum going outside, then coming back in. She's always popping in and out, to the chickens, or the compost bin, or her vegetable plot. She bakes a lot, chocolate cakes and lemon drizzle and sticky toffee puddings, and energy bars for your dad. These are things she never had time for when she was high-powered.

You're still lying on your bed wrapped up in your favourite old Teletubbies duvet when you hear your dad come into the yard on his bike, and then raised voices. He comes up to your room and he doesn't knock but barges straight in.

'Emma, there's been an accident, we're just ringing for an ambulance. Don't worry, alright? I passed it on the way back. Stay by the phone, in case the ambulance rings back. OK?

'Emma! Do you understand? We're going back with blankets. We're just on the corner of the lane. OK?

'For God's sake Emma, are you listening!?'

You don't ask who it is, or if it's serious.

Before, when you opened the door of the Mitsubishi and set off running towards home, you had no idea what would happen next. You were half-way up the track to your house, and then you heard a car skidding and the dull thud of metal on wood. You ran home as fast as you could up the lane towards your house, and when you arrived you were so out of breath you could barely speak.

You opened the kitchen door and you wanted to just run to your mum and tell her what had happened, and what you'd done. How it was all your fault. But you couldn't, and she carried on mixing whatever it was that she was mixing, and then came the usual barrage of questions: 'How was school? What did you do? Do you want some cake? I've made lemon drizzle.'

And there'd still been time then, time to tell her, and you wanted to tell her, but you had just one chance, one split second to say it. It was just a split second, and you didn't say anything, and then it was too late. It was too late to say *I think there's been an accident. I think Alan's crashed his car.*

73

Now you're lying on your bed and the ambulance is coming. Doppler-shifted, you can hear its rising siren sound.

It's your fault he crashed. You didn't even raise the alarm.

Your dad can see you've been crying when he comes in to check on you later.

'Hey, it's OK,' he says. 'Everything's fine. It was Alan, took the corner too wide. They had to cut him out, but he's fine. He'll be alright.'

Mum comes in with a cup of tea. 'The ambulance is gone. I had a chat to Alan, he's walking wounded. You were lucky, my girl. A few minutes earlier, and…'

'What did he say?' you hold your breath.

'He says he feels like an idiot. He said to tell you he's alright. He was worried how you'd take it, I guess. We'll make him a get well card, what do you think?'

You wish Alan had told them what you said, so it was all out in the open, but you're glad he hasn't, because you know it's not true, and you didn't even mean it.

Dad says, 'Makes you think, when something like this happens. Do you want to go out for a ride tomorrow? You can borrow my racing bike.'

'I don't want to race.'

'That's fine. We could all go together. How about the beach? We'll take our swim stuff. We've got to find a way to get you back into training.'

You think about putting in laps, practicing tumble turns and bilateral breathing, turning your head to one side then the other, finding a rhythm. You imagine gliding like a seal and perfecting your form.

QUARRY SWIMMING
August 2021

A dragonfly day: close-coupled, neon blue, short-lived. The pop of gorse, everything ripe too soon, the fag-end of another hot summer. We swam over secrets, the quarry water as thick and warm as sin. Sheer granite walls surrounded us, and we floated under shadowy overhanging gardens, fern-drenched and sweet with honeysuckle. I dodged a buzzard's shadow and kept my feet up, trying not to think of what might be below, while you dived down without fear. We've all seen old quarries on TV: the sawn-off shotguns and bullion, buried amongst the bones of ponies, sheep and men.

We were safe here from prying eyes. Your story: out for bike ride, such a hot day, the water too tempting to resist. Mine: a few hours' break, a neighbour popping in to check on Mum, the chance for me to do some drawing. Our alibis were over-elaborate and unnecessary; on hot days like this, everyone heads for the sea, not to the moors. We had been intoxicated, so briefly, not by each other, but by the possibilities of what we might… what we could… and the electric charge of risk, which we pretended was huge. We didn't even kiss. The risk was, in truth, infinitesimally small. Like quarry swimming, the idea was more exciting and dangerous than the truth.

You didn't stay long in the water. Spread-eagled on a granite slab, you siphoned down the heat and by the time I got out, you were sunshine-lazy and almost dry. I shivered as your hand brushed my wet shoulder, but bitter-sweet longing and regret were absent from the scene.

When I left home, she was colouring in; her hand was shaking, just a little. She gets so frustrated when she can't stay inside the lines. Even when I'm not there, I can't stop myself thinking, *I need to get back soon. She'll be waiting.*

You pretended to sleep. I knew I should leave, but instead, I climbed up to the granite outcrop above the quarry with my sketch book and pencils, following the desire path rather than the steps. The sketch book was a well-meaning gift from a newish friend – *you paint a bit, don't you?* Its blank white pages were a provocation and a dare.

On the flat of the overhang, crumpled cans circled a burnt-out fire. The kids come here, drink cider, smoke. Loud-shouting boys, legs cycling through the dead air, arms windmilling, torpedoing into the pool, looking up as soon as they surface to check that the girls are impressed. The brave girls jump too; they need less egging-on and make less fuss than the boys. I would have been one of the ones that stood and watched.

A line of cloud slanted across the quarry. How to capture that peculiar opaque absence of colour on water? And the moors beyond? A good green is the most difficult colour to mix. I imagined a canvas, roughly blocked out, and through it a gash of alizarin or vermillion; vertical, impasto, scraped back, the marks wildly made, the paint pushed out to the edge and beyond. How to bring in a different energy, something to startle, without throwing the whole scene off balance, without risking everything?

The cloud-shadow woke you. You looked up and waved, checked your watch, held both arms up in the air like an open question, then started dressing and packing yourself away. I resisted the urge to try to capture your likeness. Even as I considered this, I thought about the time I'd been away, and whether she was worried, sitting in the bay window looking out towards the sea.

I walked to the edge of the rock and looked with a dragonfly eye, 360°, slow motion, my wings folded in. I could jump, arms and legs frantically windmilling, I could make a deep gash through the hot, dead air. I could torpedo into the pool, dive deep down to the sawn-off shotguns and sacks of bullion that lie in the mud amongst the bones of ponies, sheep and men. I had never been brave enough before.

Past the mine chimneys, in the far distance, a charcoal smudge of rain over a chrome yellow hill and on the horizon, wind turbines turning slowly, slowly, slightly, just slightly out of time, cross-hatching the stubble fields below.

I should leave. I ignore the voice and open my sketchbook. Its blank pages are a welcome, a provocation and a dare.

GUILLEMOT PAYNE
October 2002

Falafel. There's always falafel in her gran's wraps; the other constituents may vary but they're always organic, and usually raw and salady. Gilly has told her gran more times than she can count not to bother doing her a packed lunch; she can always get something at College. But as Gilly runs across the landing from the kitchen to her bedroom, the tin foil package and an apple are on the table by the front door, so she can't even pretend that she hasn't seen them. She checks the hand-written label. Steamed beetroot and falafel. Great. She'll look like her hands are blood-stained this afternoon, which isn't great when you're practicing on real people's hair.

Gilly's late (she always is), and her friend Astrid is early (always, and how annoying is that?). They've got ages before the bus is due, but then Gilly looks at her watch and it's not ages at all. Gilly can hear Gran and Astrid talking in the kitchen as she unplugs her straighteners. She pauses to listen, out of habit. She never knows what Gran's going to come out with next.

'Nurdles,' Gran is saying to Astrid. 'And those cotton bud thingies, do you know how long they take to break down? No, I don't either, but it's a long time and what happens while they're breaking down?' Most old people use the Internet to look up their ailments. Gran uses it to learn eco-facts. 'Cut open a seagull and what will you find? Hundreds of pieces of plastic. Hundreds.'

'Why would you want to cut open a seagull?' says Astrid. For once, Gran is silenced. Gilly finishes putting on her mascara and joins them in the kitchen. Astrid has managed to turn the conversation towards less intense ground.

'We're on bridal and special occasions, for the next six weeks.' Astrid's been looking forward to this module since the start of the course.

'Ooooh,' says Gran. 'My favourite. I love doing the brides. Although as a feminist, I don't believe in the outmoded and shackling institution myself, obviously, but doing the hair though, lovely. Lovely, but stressful. Bride, the bridesmaids, mother of the bride, mother of the groom…'

'We're doing flower accessories…' Astrid says. Gilly grabs Astrid's arm and starts pulling her towards the door.

'Bye… Gran,' says Astrid.

'I keep telling you, call me Grace, please. I'm her gran,' she nods towards Gilly. 'Not yours. Are you doing chignons? You can't beat an up-do. Works at any age. So classy. Elegant.'

Gilly snorts. Classy and elegant is not Gran, not by any stretch of the imagination. She kept up her hippy-witch vibe, all cheesecloth and beads and ethnic skirts, well into the nineties. Gran favours the functional hiker look now, all moisture wicking, easy wash, easy dry, no iron. Even down to the khaki trousers that unzip at the knees and convert into shorts. Gilly lives in a state of almost continuous embarrassment. But at least the stinky hippy coat has been relegated to the spare room.

'Don't forget your lunch,' Gran calls after them. 'Gilly, Gilly, always in a hurry, right from the day you were born. When you popped right out…'

'Stop it, Gran!'

Gran gives Gilly the falafel wrap and an apple. 'And bring back the foil. Love you!'

'Be good, Gran.'

Gilly and Astrid escape down the stairs from the flat through the salon, it's the quickest way. Gilly tries not to look at the *For Sale* sign in the window, underneath the ghost of gold lettering that says, *Roberto's Ladies Hairdressers. No appointments necessary.*

The bus is waiting for them at the turning circle before the lane narrows to a track that leads down to the harbour. The first pick-ups on the thirty-mile ride to College, Astrid and Gilly have their choice of seats. They sit where they always sit, the back seat on the top deck. The journey is all stops and starts as they pick up other students in ones and twos from villages along the way.

'I could come and work for you. Or we could be partners.' Astrid is drawing out variations of G&A in the condensation on the window, trying out designs for their rebranded salon. 'Shabby chic. And we could have, like, a chill-out area, with leather sofas and a coffee maker.'

Gilly looks out of the window at the same trees they pass every day, the same road signs, the same pub, the same petrol station.

'We could specialise in bridal,' says Astrid into the silence. 'Or whatever you want. It's your salon. So you can choose, what do you think?'

'It's up for sale. She doesn't want me to have it. End of discussion.'

'She doesn't mean it, though.'

Grace knows that she absolutely does mean it.

The flat above the salon is the only home Gilly has ever known. The salon is Gran, and Gran is the salon. In pride of place on the wall, above the line of back basins, is a framed photo from 1967, with her gran, so young and so pretty, talking to a reporter in front of the salon door. The reporter is holding a huge microphone with 'BBC News' written on the side in an old-fashioned font. She's wearing her old afghan coat, the coat she still brings out on special occasions. She is being interviewed about the oil spill, and how they'd used the salon to clean up the seabirds. Gilly knows the story inside out. Her gran even named her Gilly, after guillemot. Most of the birds that perished had been guillemots. Gilly has always assumed that she'll leave College and join Gran in the salon.

The bus is half-full now, noisy and hot. Astrid and Gilly are older than most of the kids on the bus who are heading for the high school. From their top-row seat, they can stay aloof from the childishness around them. Astrid is still going on about Gran and the salon.

'Your gran's amazing. She's so creative. I love her driftwood things. Do you think she'd teach me?'

Gilly lets the chat wash over her. Her gran is brilliant, totally, and she can understand that she's trying to help her. But Gilly had thought they'd work together until… well, that time in the future, years away, when her gran might want to take it a bit easier. Except Gran has decided to sell the lease and put a deposit down on a small rented flat and give Gilly the rest of the money to go traveling. Gran doesn't always think. She'd honestly thought that Gilly would be delighted to get home from College one day to find a massive *For Sale* sign on what had been her home for the past seventeen years.

'She wants me to leave,' says Gilly. 'After I've finished College. When she sells up, she says she'll give me the money to go travelling.'

'What! You're kidding me. That's awesome. You're so lucky. I could come with you – when are you going?'

'I'm not,' says Gilly.

'You can't not.'

'I don't want her to sell the salon, and I don't want to go away. OK?'

'But–'

'I don't want things to change. We're fine as we are.'

Gilly knows that Astrid will never understand what it's like to have just one person in the whole universe, just one. Sometimes she feels like she's perched on a ledge on a cliff, except it's empty black space and not open blue sky in front of her.

'It's alright for you,' says Gilly. 'You've got a mum and a dad and two grans and two granddads, and cousins coming out of your ears, and ten brothers...'

'Two brothers.'

'And I've got... Well, I've got Gran. Full stop.'

'But she's awesome. Go on, admit it.'

'She's going on another march next week. She wants to get arrested.'

'Cool! My family are so boring. You're so lucky.'

'So you keep saying. Like, I'm so lucky that my mum died giving birth to me, so it's all my fault and now I have to live with an OAP.'

'You're being a cow now.'

'Sorry.'

'Forgiven.'

Gran had expected Gilly to be surprised to see the *For Sale* sign in the salon window, but happy, delighted, excited when Gran told her what she planned to do. There had been a long, empty vacuum of a moment as Gran realised that instead of being delighted, Gilly was furious, hurt, betrayed. Gilly realised that her gran had no idea how upset she'd be. The gulf of understanding between them had shocked them both. That evening, Gilly had cried more tears than she thought she had in her.

Gran had been contrite. She accepted that she'd handled it badly. But she was offering Gilly the chance to escape, to do something with her life.

'Like you wanted to?' said Gilly. 'Until you had Mum? And who said anything about travelling anyway?'

'You did. You're always planning to go off and do something. Last week, it was a rep in Magaluf. Camp America before that.'

'But I didn't mean it.'

Gran started to hum, which was always a bad sign. She chopped celery into tinier and tinier cubes. 'Anyway, I thought you hated the salon.'

'No! Sometimes. Not *hate* it.'

Gilly had helped out in the salon since she was eleven. The bit she really did hate was hooking hair out of the plugholes. The rest was OK, but whenever she and Gran argued, Gilly always bought up the subject of child exploitation, and how could her gran make her work in the grottiest, most old-fashioned hairdressers in the whole universe? Shampoo and set, perm every six weeks. *Would you like a cup of tea? Would you like an ancient Woman's Own? Last week's Radio Times to see what you've missed?*

When Gran had stopped chopping butternut squash for their curry, and Gilly had stopped crying, they sat down together at the kitchen table.

'I just want you to have the chances I didn't,' Gran said.

'Because you had me to look after when Mum died. Basically, I ruined your life. You might as well say it.'

'Just think about it, please. You're almost qualified. You could work anywhere. On the cruise ships, or in America, London, Paris, anywhere. You don't want to be stuck here – but there's no rush, there's a whole world out there.'

'I don't understand. Why do you want to get rid of me, Gran?

'I don't. Really, I don't.'

And the smell of the onions got to Gran then, and she carried on stirring the curry, her eyes red and streaming.

They've made a sort of temporary peace which means not mentioning the subject and ignoring the *For Sale* sign in the window. Gran leaves a note on the calendar by the cooker when there's going to be a viewing. Gilly tidies her room and makes sure she's not around. It's big news in the village, as they might have expected. *Have you seen? Grace is selling up. Is she staying local? Who'll be taking over I wonder?* Not many people walk past, but those that do, have a good look at the sign. People who haven't been in the salon for years, preferring somewhere a bit more modern in town, have started popping in. *Can you fit me in for a quick cut and blow dry?* It's not meant to be nosey, and they all wish Grace and Gilly well. But people do like to be the first in the know.

The bus picks up a bit of speed as they get away from lanes and onto the dual carriageway for the final leg of their journey to College. Astrid wipes a circle in the window steam, erasing her logos and salon branding, and they both look out and see the countryside passing them by. Past the roundabout, the same view as always is punctuated by a new roadside hoarding. A business park is going to be built where now there are fields. Better not tell Gran, Gilly thinks. She'll be lying in front of the bulldozers singing protest songs and all over the local six-thirty news. And everyone would be so keen to tell her that they'd seen her gran on the telly, and Gilly would be mortified, again, but proud along with it. Not everyone has an eco-warrior for a gran.

Astrid starts humming *Here Comes the Bride*, and draws love hearts on the windows.

'You are actually looking forward to doing Bridal,' says Gilly.

'Might be.'

Her gran loved doing special occasions. She loved doing anything, really – in a good way, not a stupid way. Gran had embraced punk; Gilly had seen the photos. Her mum, Joan, had been into all that, in a scaled-down, village way. Gran's back-combing skills had come into their own. 'Used to send your mum and her mates off with two layers of Elnett, but to be honest, there's not many a Mohican that'll stand up to a good Cornish mizzle.'

The bus pulls up in the College car park. They sort out their bags, stretch after being cooped up in the back seat of the bus which is really too small for them now and better fits the younger kids,

'Race you,' says Astrid, running down between the teaching blocks. 'Come on!'

Gilly chases after her, and all that matters for the next two minutes is beating Astrid to the hairdressing suite.

HOSTILE DESIGN
December 2021

He is skinny and edgy, but at least he doesn't smell of anything worse than cigarettes and too much energy. The carriage is empty, and he could sit anywhere, but he chooses her table, diagonally opposite, nearest the aisle. He tries to make eye contact as he throws his carrier bags onto the seat, sharp and quick in all his movements. Nix looks out of the window as if he doesn't exist. The train pulls away; the name of the station pulses, blurs and disappears behind them. This is a quiet compartment, and a stopping service, so she hopes he'll be silent, and soon gone.

The train speeds through tedious winter countryside, past laser-cut trees and someone else's nearly-home hills. They rock in their seats in tandem and under the bright compartment lights, they are two dark figures, one dishevelled and angular, the other sharp-pressed, also angular. The boy wears denim jacket and jeans, and a faded grey tee-shirt with a sagging neckline. She is crisp and suited, straight-shouldered, with shiny black asymmetric bob and black-framed round glasses made in Japan. The objects on the table in front of her are rectilinear and curated; Moleskine notebook, tan and saddle stitched, iPad in an understated black leather case, magazine with matt, high-concept artwork. Her colour comes from two reusable metal bottles, turquoise for decaf and fuchsia for water. She enjoys this unexpected swap of colour choices and believes that subtly reveals her playful side.

Her luggage is stowed where she can see it. One small bag contains a few multifunctional pieces that will work both for meetings and for a short stay with her sister. She hadn't originally diaried in family on this trip, but she'd had another 'You don't need to bother coming down...' call from Caro. Nix hadn't been able to get to the bottom of the problem, but it appeared their mother had suddenly stopped speaking. This was completely out of character. She decided to come down and sort it out herself; it would save her visiting again at Christmas.

'Tickets!' The conductor's voice cuts through the rhythm and hum of the train. The boy grabs his bags, and more creature than human, he's gone in the opposite direction. He leaves negative space, an imprint on the seat that slowly pushes back into its own flatness. Nix has her ticket ready for checking. The conductor rolls and pitches with the train, never missing a beat, as he moves along the aisle past the empty seats. The doors swish open, and whisper closed behind him.

She relaxes. But then the boy is back, suddenly – doors open, the smell of cigarettes, bags thrown in – and he bangs himself down into the seat diagonally opposite. She drinks from her fuchsia water bottle and flicks through screens.

'He's gone, right?'

She nods without looking up from her iPad, scared that any words or the smallest glance will be taken as encouragement by the boy – or is he a man? Somewhere on that cusp, as both her own sons are. She tries to look at him obliquely, via the incomplete back-to-front-ness of his reflection. The nerves and the edginess belong to a young man, but she can't be sure; the image of his face in the window is indistinct and shadowed, but she thinks she can make out a young softness in his features.

He starts to hum, breaks, restarts, then he's tapping his foot against the table leg. She glares. He smiles back, seemingly oblivious. How can he be? It must be deliberate. He carries on humming, nudging the table leg.

'Excuse me.' He looks up, and she indicates her notebook, her iPad. 'I'm trying to work.'

'Sorry.'

'You're banging…'

'Sorry.'

'And humming.' She always has to explain. 'You know when you're on a plane and the person behind you…'

'I'm really sorry,' he looks genuinely upset, startled even. Boy, she decides, definitely not man. He is silent, draws in his elbows, and his shoulders sink, and she wonders how anyone can reduce themselves so easily.

She carries on picking up emails, skimming, shaking her head, tutting, unaware of the noises she's making. She starts to read through her notes for her meeting later in the week. The client is a local council, so inevitably, engagement and consultation will put a strain on the budget, but with projects like these you have to be seen to be talking to all the stakeholders. She takes pride in her work; she's known for her ability to problem-solve and trouble-shoot. She starts to read through the design brief again, but she loses focus in the middle of reading, hyper-aware of the boy opposite, watching her.

As soon as she looks up, he explodes like a jack-in-a-box.

'I've never been on a plane,' he says. 'I can see how it's annoying. I get it. My mum always said I was a fidget arse. What are you doing?'

She smiles her best un-smile and returns to her iPad.

Then he's up in a flash, round the table and sitting next to her. He picks up her magazine and flicks through the pages.

'This is cool.' He runs a finger around an artist's impression of a new corporate HQ. Line drawings of people gather in a sunlit atrium under a rainforest of trees, men and women, young and old, black and white, all happy and carefully representative. The building smiles down at the people from on high.

'Are you a builder?' he says.

'I'm a designer.'

'Like Stella McCartney? Are you famous?'

She's alarmed that anyone would think she's a builder. 'I reimagine outdoor spaces,' she says. 'Street furniture.'

He opens her notebook before she can stop him.

'The DFS sale is now on...' he says.

'Public furniture. Outside.'

'Public. Furniture,' he repeats, slowly. She thinks he's being sarcastic, but he is all innocence.

He returns to her magazine, licking his finger and thumb to turn the pages. She takes a deep breath and tells herself it's only paper after all. She can buy another copy; it can be replaced. She attempts visualisation of her happy place: a calm blue sea, coral sand, no footprints.

'I suppose someone has to say – this is what it's got to look like. This is going to be made of purple plastic or metal or wood or whatever and have this sort of legs. Is it a shopping centre? Are you making a plaaa...zaaaa?' He draws the word out into something exotic.

The job is the same old, same old, trying to salvage the 1970s on a shoestring. 'Silk purse, sow's ear,' her senior partner had said, 'but sows' ears pay the bills.' A council needing to be seen to be doing something to reclaim the town centre for people to enjoy the night-time economy, without coming across rough sleepers and addicts and such like. As always, there must not be the slightest hint of deliberate hostile design. The term is toxic, she knows better than anyone. Her job is to present elegant solutions whilst neatly side-stepping the problems.

His elbow is on top of her forearm now, and she pulls away so she's right up against the cold window, but he flows over both sides of his seat and his knee touches hers and although he's so skinny he's everywhere again and leaning over the table and rummaging now for something in one of his carrier bags. He eventually finds an old-fashioned school exercise book and a Teletubbies pencil case. He's still for a minute, then again like quicksilver, 'I had a seizure.' He pulls up the sleeve of his jacket. 'Do you think this looks bad?'

She looks. The inner surface of his wrist, held out for her inspection, is pure white, blue veined, bony. A black/red gash weeps, partly scabbed, partly open.

'Christ,' she says. 'Let me...'

'It doesn't hurt. But should I go to the hospital?'

He looks at her with complete trust, as if she will have the right answer.

'Did you do this?'

'I had a seizure. I had handcuffs on, but they didn't notice my arms.'

She tries to process the scenario but can't. She looks around to see if there's anyone else in the carriage.

'The skin's all loose, look, all flappy like a fish when you land it. Do you go fishing?'

Fresh blood appears along the line of the wound, then starts to trace down his wrist where it pools then drops from his wrist onto her magazine. His blood is so like hers. She runs a finger over her own wrist, feeling its structure before she feels the pulse.

She knows there's no one in front of her in the carriage, but is anyone watching and listening behind them? Wondering what she's going to do next, what her reaction will be? She feels like she's being tested, or on some sort of TV set-up show. She looks around to check, but he doesn't notice, he's still fascinated by himself. He rolls up a discarded ticket, makes a point, and uses it to investigate the gash across his wrist and make more blood. She finds two handy packs of tissues in her bag.

She isn't equipped for situations like this. All she can bring to mind is sweet tea and smelling salts. He seems delighted by the blood that is seeping through the white of the tissue. She anxiously watches where his blood is falling in thick, fully loaded drops. She wipes her magazine, trying not to let his blood touch her fingertips.

He closes his eyes and leans back against the headrest. She waits, willing him to fall asleep. She takes a few restorative breaths to compose herself, then takes a clean tissue to turn to the article she wanted to read. Double spread artwork: concrete office block, graffiti bouncing off the walls, a kid with a skateboard, a sidebar with six boxes, street furniture, high concept, high design, nothing municipal or parks-and-gardens here.

There is a bench that will be perfect for her scheme. She wonders is she'll have time to include it in her presentation. Out of their league, financially, but so beautiful. If they see it, they might even find some more funding from somewhere.

The seat of the bench is silver and slinky, every surface rounded with the perfect mind-blowing fluidity of a Möbius loop with one seamless boundary curve. Genius. It doesn't look comfortable, but that's the whole point. It is perfect in form and function, designed to be the opposite of what it appears to be. Metal arms bisect the seat to stop anyone lying down. There is no backrest to lean against. All these features are achieved without compromising the aesthetic.

The boy shuffles awake, yawns, stretches. He opens the exercise book and starts to draw. She is unnerved by his quietness.

'Do you draw a lot?' she says.

He ignores her.

'Can I see?'

He carries on drawing.

'Let me…' she leans over to reach for the book. She means

it kindly; he grabs the book to his chest with unexpected fierceness and there's blood again.

'Leave me alone!' he shouts.

'Quiet, sssh... sssh. Hold your arm up.'

There's blood on the seat. She starts to dab. The blood hasn't sunk into the material; it settles on the stripes, as innocent as water.

'They treat the seats with something,' he says. 'Stops it staining. It looks like its soft and comfy but feel it. Go on, feel it.'

She strokes the fabric. It feels like a cheap stuffed animal and sets her teeth on edge.

He starts putting his papers and pencils back in one of his bags and pulls on his jacket. The LED announcement is on and rolling... *next stop... next stop...* The conductor's voice, *your next station stop... please make sure... mind the gap...*

'Are you going on somewhere?' she says.

'Don't be soft,' he says. 'Course I'm going somewhere.'

'I'll get off with you.'

'No thanks.'

'Is this where you live?'

'Sometimes. It depends.' He fumbles in a pocket and puts a pound coin on the table.

'It's all I've got.'

'What for?'

'Your magazine. It's messed up.'

She wants to tell him that it doesn't matter, and he needs help, and can she...? But her phone rings, she looks, it's Caro.

'I need to take this,' she says to him. 'But wait, ok? Wait.'

He's the quick, edgy person he was before, ready to run. He grabs his bags. The doors swish open.

'Yes. Five o'clock. I've got to go,' she says to her sister.

The doors whisper closed.

She watches him stop on the platform to light a roll-up, then he walks right past her window without even looking up. He sits down on the wooden bench furthest away from the waiting room, where the platform extends out into the countryside. It's getting dark already, the sky silvering towards the horizon. A few lights shine out on a distant hill.

His bags are stacked around him and it looks like he's nesting. She expects him to look up at the brightly lit carriages as the train pulls out, to look for her, acknowledge her part in his story, but he doesn't. He reaches into one of his bags and searches around, pulling out clothes like a magician and his clothes are on the bench around him, and on the floor at his feet, and he selects a jumper, but doesn't put it on. He wraps it around himself, over his jacket, half-covering his face. He pulls up his knees and drops his head and the boy in him disappears and he is just a pile of stuff, and that is the last she sees of him.

She picks up the paper he's left on his table, a couple of pages torn out from his notebook. If she were his teacher, she'd praise his mark-making and the sensitivity of the lines. She folds them and puts the sheets carefully inside her notebook.

She raises her hand and gives an uncertain half-wave as she passes the indistinct shape of him. The name of the station accelerates to a pulse, then a blur.

THE THINGS WE CAN'T SAY
August 2000

It rained on St Swithin's Day, and it's rained at least part of every day since, and it looks like it will carry on for the full forty days. A smell of damp hangs in odd corners of the farmhouse like forgotten laundry. As Rosie opens a cupboard, or fetches something from the pantry, she can smell the mustiness that only normally appears in winter. All their field gates are quagmires. Soil washes off the pasture and turns the streams brown, and the streams flow down to the coast, and there is a sweep around the harbour mouth where the run-off meets and mingles with the sea. They joke about building arks and sympathise with the holidaymakers who are making the best of it, sheltering in teashops dressed in shorts, anoraks and hastily purchased wellies.

Rosie doesn't like August. It's the month when she realises that the cycle of shortening days is well underway, and that daylight hours have been slowly slipping away from her since the June solstice and will accelerate now towards winter. Spring comes early in this part of the world, but nothing is gained and by August the fresh fizzy greens of early summer are already tired and fading. It won't be many weeks until she'll be getting up in the pitch dark to get Joe's breakfast, lighting the fire and setting the kettle on the range while he pulls on his overalls over layers of clothes, so he ends up stiff-limbed, like a scarecrow.

She dreads the coming winter. She always does. Every year is harder.

Dan sits with a mug of tea in front of him and picks away

at the jagged Formica along the edge of the kitchen table. It's hard to believe that he's a farmer's son; nearly midday and he's not even dressed yet, while Joe has already done a good six hours' work. Dan said he'd stay a week, but Rosie has already seen him checking the train times on his laptop. He usually brings friends down with him, but with the weather so bad they've all cried off this time. Joe said to her, 'That's alright, less work for you,' but it was easier with a crowd; plenty of chat, meals to cook and serve, and less opportunity for silences to form between them. She always felt compelled to fill these gaps with unnecessary words.

'Still raining,' she says. Then, with no change of tone or weight, 'I'm going to tell your father I'm leaving.' She didn't mean to say this. It's something she's been thinking about, but only in the abstract, one of a range of possible ways of pushing Joe in the direction of having a discussion with her. But now the words are out in the world, and witnessed.

The quiet that follows is like an empty church. The clock is even louder than normal, the steady tock-tock-tock rising in volume as the sound bounces back from all four walls, uninterrupted by any other noise. Rosie has to fill the void. As if he's still a child, she says, 'For goodness' sake, will you stop picking at the table. There'll be nothing left of it if you carry on like that.'

Dan runs his hand backwards and forwards across the tabletop, like he's trying to sweep away crumbs. She should be able to read him like a book, but she can't fathom his face when he looks at her. He takes after Joe in that way; she can never tell whether his head is full of really deep thoughts, or if he's just wondering what's for dinner.

Eventually he says, 'Can I ask you why you've made this decision?' Formal, slightly aggrieved, as if he's just been turned down for a job.

There isn't just one thing. There are loads of little things that don't really matter in the grander scheme, although they all have the potential to spark off like fireworks and catch into something more dangerous. But the great big, massive things – how can she talk to her son about those? The *Is this it, then? Is this the way it's going to be for the rest of my time on this Earth?* He's down on holiday for a week, probably less. These aren't the sort of conversations they're geared up to have.

'Do you want another cup of tea?' she asks.

He shakes his head, waiting for an explanation.

Rosie sits down at the table opposite Dan. Her knitting bag is on the floor next to her. She knits quickly, neatly; it's like a sixth sense, there is so much memory in her fingers. It soothes. She almost reaches in for the jumper she's working on, but then thinks that this will annoy Dan even more.

She wants to explain but hasn't got it clear in her own mind exactly what she's planning. She can tell the facts though.

'Do you know what Father does, every morning?' she says. 'He comes down at half past five, and he says to me: If I put a twenty pound note down on this table now, that's how much money I'm going to lose today. And then he has his breakfast and goes out. Into the dark, usually into the rain. It's not always the same words, or the same amount of money, but it's always something similar. Every single morning.'

'And?' Dan says. 'That's his life.'

He's right. This is Joe's inheritance, and therefore hers, as much as the canary yellow Formica-topped table that Joe's mother bought in the 1960s, an uncharacteristically extravagant and fashionable purchase. The table is now Rosie's. It sits in the kitchen where Joe's mum cooked, and where Rosie now cooks. Rosie washes the same slate floor, lights the same fire, tries to remove the stains from the same Belfast sink. The slates are uneven; Joe's mum was forever wedging newspaper under the table leg to stop it rocking. It used to drive her mad. It drives Rosie mad too.

'If it's too much for you... I suppose I could help with the paperwork or something,' says Dan.

Rosie tries not to give him the look he always accuses her of giving him. He's still sweeping imaginary crumbs off the table, but she bites her tongue. He asked her at Christmas if he could have this table. Mid-century is becoming fashionable, apparently. She'd said no, probably more out of surprise than anything. She couldn't quite believe that he would want a table – any table – let alone this one. It's hard for her sometimes to remember he's a grown-up man.

'So you're going to leave Father here on his own?' he says. 'Just like that?'

She hasn't thought it through but if she tries to explain to Dan, then it might make sense to her too.

'It won't come to that. He'll come round. It's a way of making him talk to me.'

Dan is shaking his head.

'We could sell up, pay back the bank and buy our own... I just want a small house. Modern. Somewhere I can walk to the shops. And a view. A sea view, and people, passing by, just... Is that too much to ask?'

'You've got a view.'

Rosie pushes back her chair and walks to the window over the sink. She pulls back the blue gingham curtain. 'So when I'm doing the washing up, I've got a view of mud washing off the top paddock across my yard, a broken gutter that's needed fixing for as long as I can remember, a field gate that's come off its hinges, a couple of trees that need felling, logs that need splitting before the winter...'

She stops suddenly, surprised by the shrillness in her voice.

'And you want – what? – A box on an estate somewhere?

He'd hate that. You'd hate that.'

'Would I?'

'Why don't you just talk to him? What's the matter with you two?'

There's no doubting the look on her son's face now. She can't blame him.

'It would be different if...'

'If what?' he snaps, wary now.

'Nothing.'

But it's not nothing. It would be different if Dan planned to move back, sometime. If she thought the farm would stay in the family, or if he'd ever said anything about settling down, as something he'd like to do, not yet maybe, but in the future.

It would be different if Dan visited more often, not just when he had nowhere better to go in the holidays. If this wasn't just somewhere to bring his friends for the weekend.

It would be different if Dan had any sort of interest in the farm – but he doesn't, never has had, and probably never will.

She wouldn't say any of those things to Dan, ever. Perhaps it would be better if she did, but there are things that just get said without thinking, and there are things that will never reach the point of being spoken.

None of this is Dan's fault, or his responsibility. She wants to apologise, but the words don't come to her.

The clock strikes the hour, like a gothic prop. Dan's cup is empty. He's picking away at the worn-out edge of the kitchen table again. Rosie can't stand the silence and the reflex kicks in: 'So – do you want another cup of tea yet, or shall we wait 'til Father comes in?'

Dan pushes his chair back from the table and leaves the room, closing the kitchen door quietly behind him. She wishes he would slam the door, or even shout. He's probably upstairs in his room, checking train times again. Rosie knows he'll side with his father, if sides are to be taken.

Rosie walks round and tucks Dan's chair back under the table. Usually she'd do this without thinking, but today she notices. She sweeps her own imaginary crumbs off the table and bends down to reposition the newspaper that's wedged between the leg and the slate.

Outside the rain is sheeting down, and water is flowing from the fields above the farmhouse, over the concrete, in wave, after wave, after wave. It's like all of their soil is heading for the sea. Joe is in the top field, she can see the tractor with the seagulls following, drawn inland by bad weather. He'll be wet through, poor bugger. Wouldn't he prefer to be doing something else?

She's not certain what she's done today, whether damage has been done, and whether she's committed to threatening a course of action that she really doesn't want to go through with. Words have come out of her that she didn't know she wanted to speak. She's said all she had to say, but to the wrong man, implicating her son, when she should have been talking to his father.

She loves Joe. This is one of those big, massive things that doesn't need to be spoken; she loves her husband, and she knows he loves her. Is it wrong for her to want something more?

They inherited the kitchen clock along with the farm and everything else. It was Joe's mother's, probably her mother's before her. It's dark oak and brass, old fashioned and ugly. But it keeps good time. Rosie can only just lift it down from the mantelpiece. She carries it outside into the yard and stands it up in the rain, against the mossy wall of the old shippen, right under the gutter that's been leaking for years. The building hasn't been used for anything but storage since Joe's uncle Samuel was alive. He used to come down from London to write his books there. The gutter's been leaking so long that there's a groove in the concrete where the water's made its own channel to the drain.

In Joe's parents' times, rabbits and pheasants would be hung under the eaves, fur and feather interleaved. And blue-black crows, wings out like witches. When he was fencing during the winter, Joe's dad would nail a dead crow upside down on a post: more use than a scarecrow, he'd say, and a darn sight more satisfying.

Rosie runs back inside, grateful for the warmth of the Aga. Joe will be out for hours yet, worrying over the rain and what'll happen to this year's harvest. But he'll see the clock when he gets back, propped up by the shippen, and he'll know something's not right. If he asks what's happened, she hopes she'll be able to tell him.

There are words she wants to share about change and about happiness. She'll practice now what she needs to say, so that strange words don't appear in the space between them. She wants the right words to come out into the world, and to be witnessed.

DROWNING IN GREEN
December 2021

She takes up so much more air and space in my cottage than you'd think from the small, self-contained neatness of her. As soon as Nix dismisses the taxi and walks through the front door, we are diminished. Mum slumps even further into herself, and I battle a fight-or-flight response. Nix doesn't look like she's just spent five hours on a train. She is completely uncreased. I'm wearing old jeans and a man's hoodie. Why didn't I even think to put on something – if not smart – at least interesting. I put the kettle on the range.

'Tea?' I ask. Mum's heard, I can tell, but doesn't answer.

'Hello, Mum.' Nix squeezes past the kitchen table. The armchair faces out to the garden, and takes up most of the small, curved bay window. Nix tries to kiss her on the cheek, except there's not much space, and Mum's staring out of the window, half turned away, ignoring everyone, and Nix sort of misses.

Although on the surface Nix looks like her normal, spick and span self, there's something tired, almost deflated about her. Probably no-one else would notice; she always appears so unstoppable.

We sit at the kitchen table. Nix calls home but it's obvious she doesn't expect an answer and she leaves a short message to say she's arrived. I ask her how her journey had been, and she shakes her head and says she'll tell me later.

'So what does the doctor say? About…' Nix nods towards our mother.

'I haven't…'

Nix can sigh louder than anyone I know.

'It's good of you to come,' I say. 'But there's no panic.'

'Really?'

'I just thought you should know.'

'Thank you.'

We are always polite to each other. There's a fragility in our relationship that won't stand up to much pressure.

I pick up her small but surprisingly heavy case and carry it up to my bedroom, trying to pretend it's as light as a feather, and that there's no problem at all getting the suitcase round the awkward kink in the staircase. Nix follows me, and I dare her to comment on the narrowness of the stairs, or anything else, for that matter. She doesn't offer to sleep on the sofa.

There are three small canvases propped up on the shelf opposite the foot of my bed. I'd meant to move them before she arrived. The canvases are unframed, unfinished, vulnerable; I wish I'd at least put a sheet over them. They all need – something – a different energy, something to startle, but there's the risk of ruining what I've already put down. This problem is so urgent and compelling, I'm picturing how this might work and…

'Hello! Wakey wakey! Where are your spare hangers?'

I layer even more shirts and jumpers over dresses and skirts to free up some hangers and squash my things along the wardrobe rail.

'Is this what you're working on?' She gives each canvas a quick once-over. 'Have you sold anything lately?'

'It's difficult to work. With Mum.'

'Really? I thought it would be ideal. All this time on your hands, you don't know how lucky you are.' I bridle, ready to fall into the habit of taking offence, but she seems to be genuinely concerned.

Two of the canvases are abstracted spring hedgerows, exercises in green, a recurring preoccupation. The third is a departure for me; a traditional landscape, a study in the palettes and tones of melancholy and yearning, although this hadn't been the intention for it.

'You're so talented,' she says. 'You need to make time.' She pulls her glasses down off the top of her head. 'That's the quarry,' she says. 'Up on the moor.'

I'm surprised she remembers. Years ago, before I moved down here, we camped on a farmer's field near there, our tents hunkered down below the stone walls. Mark and I were invincible then. We found Ferry Cottage, our dilapidated dream, and moved down shortly after. Nix thought we were stupid and told us so. She's always had an urban heart.

I sold Ferry Cottage ten years ago, when I finally accepted that I'd never fix up our dream on my own. There had been a slow realisation that with every passing year, the list of jobs that needed doing was stretching into something frightening. This house is nearer the sea, and smaller than Ferry Cottage; if I'd thought that Mum would move in, I might have looked for something larger.

Nix has only brought a few things, she's made it clear she can't stay long – a few days, then she has to head off to a meeting.

'So how's she been, generally?' she says, when she's tidied her things away.

I tell her that Mum had been her usual self; garrulous, gossipy, embarrassing, marvellous for her age, mischievous, infuriating. But then she'd started somehow to be less than that, in small, and barely noticeable ways that taken together, added up to a difference.

'Do you think she's got…?'

I don't let her finish. 'I think she's homesick,' I say. 'This refusing to speak… I don't know, it's about control. I think.'

There's a beat while Nix digests this. Mum's been saying quite a lot over the last few months that she wants to go back to London. She doesn't like it here.

'And there was nothing more… nothing that brought it on?'

I think that's the whole point. There is absolutely nothing going on here, and Mum misses the hustle and bustle of her old life. Peace and quiet, beautiful scenery and bucolic charm just aren't her style. When we moved her down here, we didn't give this blindingly obvious fact a second thought.

Mum has nodded off in her chair. Nix takes a cup of tea and crouches by her side. I'm touched by her gentleness. I manage to make Nix so strident and bossy when she's absent; it fits my picture of her to be the organiser, the sorter-out of family woes. I don't always give the rest of her character enough credit.

'What's all this nonsense then?' she says.

Mum takes the tea, the cup slightly shaky in the saucer, but doesn't answer.

Nix straightens up and looks out of the window. I join her, and we are squashed into the alcove together, a family tableau, elderly mother and her daughters looking out of the window into the distance. I can't resist placing one hand on Mum's shoulder, and the other on Nix's forearm; we're too close together to make a perfect composition, but the circle we make, and the difference in our standing and seated heights, are pleasing to the eye.

It's a bright afternoon, and I let my gaze follow the line down the path, to the diagonals of the gate, past the low stone wall, and beyond to fresh growth on the fields like a very fine pinstripe, and the fields folding away down the valley. A triangle of sea is cushioned between the hill-pillows, and the sky is flat, like a child's painting.

'Shouldn't you get a lock on that gate?' Nix says.

Mum has her tea on a tray; ham salad, jacket potato, it's something she enjoys. She goes to bed early, taking herself off without a word, and I can see that Nix is struggling to deal with this silent version of her mother, who usually has so much to say.

Nix has started to unwind. She's on the sofa, hugging her legs like a teenager. Nix turns her nose up at pizza but eats it all the same. We start on the first bottle of prosecco to celebrate nothing in particular. Nix tells me about a boy she met on the train, a rough sleeper she thinks, and she seems at a loss for an opinion about this boy and how he lives, and watching her, I realise again how much softer she is than she appears.

I tell her about my work and the lack of progress, and at some point in the evening, I tell her about the man who was a mistake. She tells me about her pride in raising the boys on her own and her achievements at work. At some point in the evening, she tells me how trapped she feels, and I have to walk away. We manage to talk about Mum without once addressing the subject.

The following morning, I take Nix tea in bed. She tells me she's decided she's not going to get up, ever. For a moment, as she lies in my bed, the duvet scrunched round her, pink pyjamas, no make-up, I feel like I'm the older sister.

'Paracetamol?' In our younger days, we wouldn't have been floored by two bottles of prosecco and a margherita pizza.

Nix doesn't surface for another hour. Her asymmetric bob needs precision to function, and she's not pulled it off this morning.

'Those pictures gave me nightmares,' she says. 'I dreamt I was drowning.'

Mum appears, washed, dressed and smiling brightly.

'Morning Mum,' says Nix, not shouting, but close enough, and not expecting an answer.

'Morning,' Mum says. 'Is breakfast ready? Always have a fry-up when we've got visitors. How are the boys? Tell me what they're up to.'

Nix announces that we are to have a family meeting.

'We should set some ground rules,' she says, and then catches the look that Mum shoots across the kitchen table towards me.

'Do you want to go first, Mum?' I wonder whether Nix is going to suggest that I take minutes or something. Mum frowns and there's a long pause while she gathers what she's going to say.

'I want to go back to London. I thought it would be like it used to be... you know. People going up and down the street, and cars, and bikes... things to watch, people to wave to, I suppose...'

'You've got such a lovely view from here,' says Nix to Mum, as if she's a stranger.

'If you like grass.'

'You can watch the birds.' At least Nix is trying.

'I never see a soul. I've got no-one to talk to.'

'Except me,' I say, trying not to sound annoyed.

'Nothing to see but fields. I miss seeing people going about their business.' Mum's found her groove. 'Postman. Milkman. Anyone really.'

'By why the not talking?' says Nix. 'What's that all about?'

'You're listening now, aren't you?' says Mum.

The back and forth continues, Nix telling Mum why she's better off here. There's a line of cloud out towards the sea, and the land-side sky is like pale blue porcelain, but out over the water it's an almost inky black, and if you were to truly capture that other-worldly skyscape in paint, people would say – that's so unrealistic, you'd never see a sky like that.

'But if Caro can't manage, I suppose we could think about... Caro? For God's sake!'

'Of course I can manage.' Or did I say – *of course I can't?* Whichever it was, I think I shouted.

'Do you have any idea what it's like living in London now?' Nix continues, softening her voice, in retreat. 'We want you to be happy, of course we do, but the practicalities. And it's so much better for you here.'

The previous evening's alcohol is still hollowing out my head and my stomach, and it's taking all my energy to resist the temptation to lie down on the sofa and be lulled into sleep by their voices. Nix is getting louder, Mum softer.

'...and I can't have you,' says Nix, at some point. 'Obviously. Not with work, and the boys. And it's not as if Caro's got a proper job.'

Now that Mum is speaking again and the question of moving back to London has been dismissed, Nix decides that she'll bring forward the meeting with her client which means leaving this afternoon. She'll stay in a hotel overnight and go straight to their offices in the morning. I carry her case back downstairs where it waits to escape by the front door.

'You're not going already?' Mum's getting teary, on the verge. 'Will you bring the boys next time?'

'You can always come and visit us, when the boys are down from Uni.'

'Christmas?' says Mum, and the hope in her voice breaks my heart. Nix disappears upstairs to check she's not forgotten anything.

'I need you here at Christmas,' I say, trying to jolly things back to safer ground. 'Who else is going to help me burn the turkey?'

Mum smiles, but she's shrinking away again, down into her chair, down into herself. When she cries, it comes without effort, like a small leak or overspill. Her tears dry quickly, yellow-crusty on her face. I squeeze her hand and kiss the top of her hair. 'Sorry, Mum,' I say. 'We'll go up and visit them soon, I promise.'

I've offered to take Nix back to the station. She'd probably prefer a taxi but can't think of a reason to refuse. I carry her case out to the car and wedge it in the back.

'If I can't come to you, why don't you come here for Christmas?' says Mum. 'We'll manage. The boys can sleep on the floor, they won't mind.'

Nix laughs as if she's said something funny and kisses her goodbye. She makes contact this time. Mum opens her book of colouring in, as if she's making a point. It upsets her that she can't always stay inside the lines.

They're clearing the drains in the lane and Nix almost misses her train. She runs ahead to open the door; I follow with the case. We don't have time to worry about whether to kiss or hug. Train doors hiss shut. She doesn't hear me blurt out, 'I'm doing my best,' and so she doesn't have the chance to say, 'I know.'

Nix opens the window and shoves an envelope at me. It's not sealed, and I lift the flap. Crisp ten pound notes, straight from the machine. I watch as she settles herself at a table, organising her magazine and papers. As the train pulls out of the station, she waves and then I realise I'm clutching ten pound notes and waving them at my sister, like a tic-tac man just before the off, or a desperate semaphore operator as the Ship goes down.

One by one, I release the bank notes. Nix is waving but not watching. She doesn't witness the warm train-wind catching and lifting them into the sky where they hang in the air for a moment before spiralling down towards the platform like sycamore seeds. No-one knows what to do – help retrieve them, or pretend it's not happening. I'm laughing, so they leave me alone.

The few people left on the platform have that deflated, turning-away look that signals that they've just said goodbye. The train accelerates towards its vanishing point, a perfect lesson in perspective.

CREAM CAKES AT THE KNIT AND NATTER
July 22nd 2022

Rosie stops off for cream cakes on the way into the Centre. She sets up the room the way they like it – close enough to talk without shouting, but with enough space for bags of wool, and tapestry hoops and all their outpourings of creative paraphernalia. While she waits for her ladies, she opens her birthday cards. She leaves the one from Joe until last. Soppy rhymes. She doesn't approve, but he's written 'all my love' in his awkward, farmer's hand, and knowing without doubt that he does love her, still, she looks forward to the coming day with a joyful heart.

The Community Centre stands on the edge of the new estate above the village, with a distant stripe of sea to the front, and a view across felted fields and farmsteads out to the moor behind. It's a blocky, awkward quilt of a building that serves the community around the harbour and the outlying villages, providing space for people to do whatever people in the community want or need to do, and whilst it's not the best-looking building in the world, murals and posters, flags and bunting all do their bit to brighten, bolster and beautify.

The Council donates the room to them for free; Rosie and her ladies are *Outreach,* apparently. In return, they're sent a constant thread of visiting speakers, liaison officers and coordinators for this and that. It stops the ebb and flow of their chat, and Rosie tries to put them off, but it's the price they have to pay for a free room and a cup of tea. A man came in last Wednesday: *How do you feel about poverty in the old? Are you claiming all you should? And winter fuel allowance?*

That must help? They're all nice enough these people, and well meaning, but Rosie knows they haven't got a clue. Two weeks ago, a woman with big hair and veiny legs. *Could you yarn bomb the town?* She showed them photos of crochet-covered lampposts and daisies on railings. *Other towns have won awards for civic stuff like this,* she said. So Rosie said – *What happens when it rains? Some of the ladies here are old enough to remember knitted swimsuits, and the sag.* That got a laugh. A shame to put the dampers on it; she was so sure that her project would be good for them. No-one seems to get the message; they're all perfectly happy to just knit and natter.

The Community Centre does a lunch for them in winter, and very welcome it is too, especially for the older ones. Soup, tinned tomato, Value Range. It has a faint metallic tang, but no-one complains, it hits the spot. The volunteers do their best with what they've got, which is diddly squat, sweet FA of not a lot.

The ladies arrive in their usual order; the ones who are always early are early; the ones who are invariably late are late, arriving breathless and flustered as they always do, with a funny story to tell of a minor drama along the way.

Rosie gets out her current project, a waistcoat, plain knit. You can't have too many. She's using wool unpicked from one of Joe's old cardies, embracing the trend for recycling. They used to do Creative Textiles with a proper teacher until Adult Ed bit the dust. They had explored themes and dabbled in mixed media. They were big on seascapes and ruined engine houses. Until it moved inland, they exhibited once a year at the library. Rosie doesn't miss all that. They all get on with their bits and pieces. Baby clothes used to be the thing, but the young mums don't want them now. Rosie is thankful that crocheted doilies have had their day. And socks too. Who nowadays can turn a heel? Isn't that something that sailors used to do?

Rosie isn't sure how she came to have Joe's cardigan; it

was just one of those things that had ended up in the wrong place when she left the farm. After so many years of marriage, a straight line of separation had been difficult to draw, and it had taken a while for their belongings to settle. She had taken too much with her to the flat on the estate, not really comprehending her new spatial realities. Things she thought she needed – spare pillows and blankets, a preserve pan, a stock pot – had to be sent back with Dan to the farm, to be placed back in the empty spots that awaited their return.

Most of the ladies at Knit and Natter are on their own, or caring for husbands who are chair bound, bed bound or just plain lost. For some of them, this is their only time to themselves. Rosie is the only one who's separated. She and Joe never got round to divorce. Neither of them had the stomach for it, and it seems like they're courting again now; although that's not quite the word that Rosie would use for it. But whatever 'it' is that they're doing, it involves meeting up and going out. Joe's taking her into town for dinner tonight, a birthday treat. She's booked to have her hair done but is having second thoughts; she doesn't want to seem like she's trying too hard. She feels that she's hovering on the verge of being ridiculous, but it's as if they're having the romance they never had when they were young, when there was no money, and work to be done on the farm seven days a week, and all they could manage was the Friday night dance in the Church hall if he wasn't working, or an evening down on the beach, with fish and chips, and sand in her hair.

A lot of her ladies would come here every day if they could, especially in winter, on those days when they can't seem to get warm indoors, and the meter spins around in free fall like it has nothing better to do. Rosie has thought about asking the Council person if they could meet more than once a week over the winter, but she doesn't like to push her luck, or come across as needy.

They're breaking up for summer next week. Some will have the grandkids down; some will go up-country to their relatives. When they meet up again after the summer, you should hear the noise, like school kids in a playground, so much to tell, catching up on the knit and purl of each other's lives, the details and the patterns, the dropped stitches, the knit two together, and all the gossip in between. But after summer visits from family, and the chance to have that chat, the chat that is almost always overdue, inevitably, some decide to leave. They depart for granny annexes near their families, moving on from their beloved retirements by the sea. Sometimes Rosie is relieved. Nobody wants to be – well, lumbered – no, that's unkind. No one wants to be responsible for someone who's going downhill – not when most of them are teetering near the top of that particular slippery slope themselves.

There's something restful about a room full of women, sitting and chatting and knitting along together. The routine, the quick fingers, the simple pleasure in making. All in all, they're a happy group. There's a bit of back-biting, of course, there always is. But Rosie always makes sure there's a fuss on birthdays; everyone gets a pile of cards to open. It's important to count the cards, to tell the grandkids when they ring.

I had twenty seven cards from my friends, can you believe? So it doesn't matter that you didn't… Of course not, you're busy, it doesn't matter… Young people lead such busy lives these days.

Dan runs the farm now, with his wife and the kids. They've converted the shippen for Joe, who has promised not to interfere. Rosie doesn't see much of the family since she moved out, not surprising in the circumstances and with so much work to be done around the farm. Dan's wife wouldn't want her hanging around anyway; the farmhouse is hers to run now. There was never any acrimony, just incomprehension that she was really going to leave, puzzlement that was left unvoiced.

There was no lack of love, just her need – selfish perhaps – to stir things up, to try on a different sort of life for size. It wasn't a mistake, and she has no regrets. But Joe's card, his 'all my love', brings her the lightness of heart she didn't think she'd feel again, and perhaps this has been the true gift of her leaving.

They stop work after an hour or so for cream cakes and sherry, as they always do on birthdays. Her ladies make a fuss of her. Everyone remarks how well she looks, and how does she manage it? She's looking younger and younger every day.

STRANGE WATERS
July 22nd 2022

The day the fin whale died, social media was full of sad and crying faces, and there was anger about ghost nets, nurdles and the like. The whale was sixty feet long, and thin, deflated. People lined up along its flanks. They poured water over it, stroked it, tried to coax it back to life with gentle singing. There was weeping.

After the heatwave in the spring, came the thirty-day monsoon at the start of summer, that washed the land into the sea. Now, although there had been an almighty storm the previous night, the day was calm and innocent, like days used to be, and it was hard not to view the beached whale as an omen.

Joe had been the first person to see it. He'd thought at first it was the Germans landing, some sort of left-over confusion from a dream of the previous night about the barbed wire that was still buried in the sand dunes, protecting the coastline from invaders. In his dream, the barbed wire and wartime concrete defences had all been exposed by ferocious weather.

He drove down from the farm to clear his head with a good blast of sea air. Although he was retired, Joe still had the habit of early rising and the beach was deserted except for a few other dog walkers on the far end of the sand nearest the harbour. The surf that morning was lifeless, exhausted. The previous night's storm had shifted the beach again, and another section of the cliff below the coast path had come down, exposing more fresh earth like an open sore.

Joe stood on the strand line and his old collie barked his lungs out at the sea; the dog missed working, the same as he did, and was always trying to herd anything he could. The dog suddenly dropped to the sand, ears up, head to one side, alert. Joe didn't see anything at first, but then a shadow, something solid, bulky, just breaking the waves. His first thought – a U-boat, or a landing craft; then – was it that tanker that broke on the reef? Not that either, much stranger; a whale that had stranded.

That afternoon, he went to the town museum. He found a blurry postcard of the tanker, and some pictures, and a short description inside a display case. At the time there had been so much coverage on the TV and in the papers, there must be lots of material available somewhere and he thought he might start a bit of a local history project, something to keep him occupied now that he was supposed to be keeping out of the day-to-day working of the farm. It would be interesting to look back and find out properly what had happened.

On the way home from town, he passed a dead crow nailed upside down to a wooden post. He hadn't seen that for donkeys' years; it was something his dad used to do.

*

Chloe had a couple of hours between shifts. She wanted to paddle, that was all, and be on her own. Instead, she sat on the sand-slope above the beach where the whale had stranded, sorting through the tiny pieces of pastel-coloured plastic that were pick-and-mixed with the sand. She examined each iridescent shell that she came upon. They looked like tiny baby's fingernails and she laid them out carefully in a line.

She ignored the people sand-scrambling past her towards the whale. She ignored the cars and vans on the lane behind, and the TV cameras, the people in high-viz jackets, the people taking selfies, the people with ropes and buckets; and the jet skis and the RNLI and the Coastguard's RIB and two Land Rovers drawing flowers on the sand, and someone with a megaphone.

*

Down on the beach, Gilly was helping to deliver sandwiches and flasks of tea to the volunteers who were trying to keep the whale alive. She was leaving the village the following day. This was a chance to say good-bye to anyone she might have missed, and a good way to leave, helping out. *I'm not leaving forever,* she laughed, *I'll be back. You can't get rid of me as easily as that!* Everyone in the village had an opinion about what she was doing. Some said, *How could she leave now? Grace isn't getting any younger.* Others said, *Why shouldn't she? She's a grown woman, I'd get away if I could.*

On top of the dunes, on the other side of the bay, away from all the uproar, Grace watched a gannet drop from the sky, barrelling into the sea. There'd been a time when Grace hadn't known one sea bird from another and had no idea of their ways or their names. Out of habit, she picked up some stones and made a small cairn for Joan; never a day passed without thought of her. She kissed the top stone and put it in place, and gave thanks for Gilly, her Guillemot, named after the first bird that she had saved.

Grace couldn't imagine how life would be without Gilly. A job in a hotel in London: Grace was excited for her, and scared, and worried. Gilly wasn't a teenager anymore, afraid to fly from the nest, but a grown woman, and this was the right thing for her to do.

Grace stood on the top of the dunes and wedged her foot against a thick hummock of marram grass to stop herself slipping. The wind was keen, and she pulled her old afghan coat around her. She wasn't sure why she'd brought it out with her today, perhaps it was because of Gilly's departure.

Some of the surfers had already given up on the blown-out waves. They stood by their cars in the car park behind her, wetsuits stripped down and hanging from their hips, exposing raw pink and blue-white skin, like they'd been skinned alive, the flesh startling against black neoprene. Some of the surfers were still lined up in the swell, unconcerned about fin whales and rescues and omens. They looked to the horizon. Still hoping for the perfect wave. The next wave will be awesome... it'll be great tomorrow, the day after, next week... Next year I'm off to the west coast of Ireland, California, Hawaii, Finisterre...

Grace remembered how they used to all come to the beach, when they were young and lithe and sleek as dolphins. This had been their everyday heaven. They'd had no idea how lucky they were. All she'd wanted to do was get away to somewhere else, where more exciting things happened. In her memory, after the sea, hungry and buzzing, they'd dance round camp fires built of driftwood. That was a trick, it was only a few times. She could hardly swim and if she went into the sea, she'd always ended up frozen stiff and it was home for a hot bath, dumping sand and strands of seaweed across her mother's carpet, and her tutting at the sand but more at Grace for having nothing better to do.

Around the rocky fringes of the bay, half a dozen seals were balanced, half-moons perched on small pillows of rock, only visible because of their constant shuffling and adjusting. Grace slipped off the coat which carried the marks and stains of a whole lifetime, and a circular burn like a brand from her homestead. She dropped it at the foot of a spindly Tamarisk tree. Sinking her heels into the soft silver sand, she let her weight dislodge the sand below, and for a moment, she was poised and then a small collapse below her, and an avalanche, and she tipped forward, running, toppling forward, and her legs couldn't keep up, and she fell, all angles and awkwardness, and thought, *You're too old for this!* She lay on her back, wondering when she'd last laid back and just watched the big sky. She wondered who would pick up the coat.

117

In the hinterland, between the sea and the moors, and up on the estate above the village, people watched the helicopter circling. Must be another rescue, they thought, until they saw on the news that a fin whale had stranded.

Caro walked the two miles down from the cottage. The first day without rain for so long but the lane was still puddled and the hedgerows flattened. She hadn't heard the news and she was surprised at the number of cars that passed her. She wondered whether it was the just a change of weather that had bought everyone out for the day. She heard a cycle bell behind her, and a family swished past – father, mother, teenage daughter. The woman shouted something cheerily as she passed that was probably hello! The man raised his arm in what could have been an open question.

At the beach, Caro sketched, excited by so many people, and so much movement, and so much energy. Her pencil seemed to flow with a life of its own. She tried to capture everything in the broadest strokes, and sat, absorbed in her task, looking down on the people milling around the dark bulk of the whale, and the boats and the jet-skis that patterned the water. Caro wondered if she might do some good work, and soon; she felt that tension and itchiness growing in her belly. It felt like a new start. She had already made a list of what she'd like to achieve, and everything today seemed possible. And if she could sell some work – that would be even better; she couldn't ignore the fact that she could do with the money.

*

Although she had been distracted by all the activity on the beach, Gilly needed some time on her own. The thought of saying goodbye to her gran sat like a rock in the pit of her stomach and she left the volunteers and wandered off towards the black open mouth of the sea-cave. Gilly had forgotten how the temperature dropped as soon as you entered, and the air seemed to lose its taste and smell. She squeezed into the small, damp chamber at the very back of the cave, grazing her shoulder on a jagged piece of slate. Soft, yellow light came down from a hole in the roof, which led, not to the outside world, but to a shaft that opened up in the kitchen floor of the house built on the rocks above. When people were in the kitchen, you could stand in the chamber and look up and see their feet.

The house had been a B&B for years. Before she left school, Gilly used to clean there in the summer holidays and serve breakfasts when the regular housekeeper needed help, and when Gran could spare her from the salon. The guests fell into two groups; those who walked across the glass panel in the kitchen floor, and the ones who skirted round the edge. Gilly always edged around the glass, never walked over it. There was no-one up in the kitchen today. She squeezed back out of the chamber and climbed up the worn steps to the raised ledge above the cave floor. The tide would be coming in soon. She knew that if she stayed much longer, she'd be trapped until the tide turned.

*

Chloe ran down the sand-slope, leaving the lines of shells behind her. She moved right into the middle of the throng surrounding the whale and joined the people who were lined up along its flanks.

After a while, she left the whale, intending to go into the sea-cave, but she saw that Gilly was there ahead of her, so Chloe walked past and sat on the rocks. Chloe and her friends used to hang out along the harbour wall or down here on the beach all the time. A few years ago, they came down to the cave every day in the summer, although they probably didn't, she just remembers it that way. She closed her eyes and remembered the rounded steps that led up to a large, flat ledge above the cave floor. They used to sit with their legs hanging over the drop as the tide thundered in and hit the walls of the cave, squealing as icy sea water splashed over them. Once the tide was in, you were trapped until it turned, but it was safe up on the ledge. They used to sing in there, playing with the echo.

Chloe wrote a poem about the dying whale. Sometime afterwards Noah set it to music, and everyone from the village learned it.

Because the summer's storms had been so fierce, the base of the cliffs had been pounded and it was possible, even after fifty-odd years, to smell oil, quite distinctly, over and above the smell of the whale.

There was still oil in the old quarries, here and in the Channel Islands. When they bombed the slick, they created millions of uncatchable drops; they didn't know any better then. The whale stank. An expert identified it as a sub-adult female. The smell didn't stop people sitting by her side and singing, but it was too late, and the whale was pronounced dead. Everyone knew it was inevitable, but still, there was shock.

*

Joe was at home getting ready to go out for the evening when he heard it announced on the radio. He was taking Rosie out to dinner for her birthday, like a date, he supposed. It felt so strange, yet so normal; after all, they'd been married so many years. He wondered what he should wear, he didn't want to appear foolish or as if he was trying too hard. He was planning to ask Rosie if she'd move back in with him, if he managed to keep his nerve. It felt like the right time. He'd kept his promise to Dan not to interfere in the farm, and he and Rosie would be able to do whatever they wanted, it was never too late.

On the mantelpiece in the shippen, a wooden bowl cradled the pieces of sea-glass that Rosie used to collect. Frosted blues and greens, mermaids' beads. She left them behind when she moved out of the farm. Joe tipped them out and rolled them between his palms, wondering why he'd never really looked at them before, and why he hadn't paid more attention.

*

Gilly sat on the ledge and tried to work out how long until the next low tide; she didn't think she'd be able to get out until the early hours of the morning. She could just imagine what her gran would say, but in the meantime, she curled up and waited. She didn't think she'd ever been here on her own before. The cave was bigger than she remembered, and dark. The light from the cottage glowed around the entrance to the farther chamber, but it just made her darkness seem even darker, and more like a living thing. She would be leaving the village tomorrow, and leaving her gran, her rock, her everything – not forever, but somehow it felt like it. She wasn't sorry that she was trapped in the cave; she wasn't too old to want to hide for a while.

Gilly thought that her skin had started to smell of the sea again; the clean, unvegetated air of the cave confirmed it. It's not unusual, her gran had said, goes with the territory, I'm afraid. She'd been born with it, like so many had, the saltiness passing down the maternal line. But it had faded away as she toddled into childhood and disappeared completely as she lurched into her teenage years, when all she smelled of was the foundation and blusher that she used to cover occasional outbreaks of itching, flaking skin. The products she used only made her skin worse. Sitting in the sea-cave, she wondered how she would be, living away from the sea for the first time, and whether it would even be possible.

*

The authorities tried to float the body out at high tide. But in the end, they had to start cutting the carcass up and take it away in trucks. The police were there in force, and volunteers with whistles, trying to keep sightseers away but still there were pictures posted up by people with drones.

They were clearing away all the equipment that had been used in the rescue when Grace came down, asking if anyone had seen Gilly. The light was fading, and the sea was starting to sharpen the white of its surf. People were still talking in small groups, reluctant to leave the scene. Chloe said she thought she'd seen Gilly going into the sea-cave but that was ages ago, before the tide came in.

When strange things happen in one place, in rapid succession, events can get confused in the public's mind. *Isn't that where…? The same place…? Are you sure…?*

How had the fin whale got so far off course? Was it alone or were there more? Everyone had a theory; climate crisis, ghost nets, ship-strikes and acidified water were all blamed, despite the post-mortem that settled on natural causes. People were shocked, upset, angry at the tragedy of the whale.

*

Joe was surprised at the reaction, when so many small, everyday human sadnesses went by unnoticed. Joe knew that things just happened sometimes, there wasn't always an easy explanation for everything. He wondered whether the whale had simply had enough. Adrift in strange waters, alone, had she lost her bearings, and exhausted, thought – here's a place to rest, a good place?

It rained again that night, sending torrents through abandoned mine shafts and washing more land off the saturated fields, down overflowing culverts and streams. The storm came in straight off the sea. Once the harbour wall was breached, it was all over in an hour or two; the village destroyed, the beach gone except for a thin shingle ribbon at high tide. The sea-cave was submerged and lost forever.

ANOTHER PLACE
March 2032

Dan drove slowly along the coast road, disorientated by patches of fog that suddenly descended and then cleared in some confusing rhythm that he couldn't quite catch or settle in to. He almost missed the familiar iron gates and had to turn in sharply, the wheels of his car spitting gravel. Nearly every window in the building was filled with bright yellow light, as if as many lamps as possible had been switched on in order to keep the gloomy afternoon at arm's length.

The building wore its history on its sleeve; block-built extensions, fire doors and metal fire escapes revealed its progression from merchant-built family home, through wartime hospital, and then children's home, to its current use as a care home.

Wouldn't you prefer somewhere modern? Purpose built? Dan rehearsed what he was going to say to his dad. Not fit for purpose, uneconomical, unsustainable; no-one could argue with the cold, precise words that described the truth of the building.

A flimsy-looking, single storey sun-room ran along the whole width of the front façade, lined with wing chairs and coffee tables, where, on brighter days, residents and visitors could chat and enjoy the sea view, or nod in the sunshine, heads hanging down like winter Hellebores.

Dan looked up, knowing that Joe would be standing at one of the metal-framed windows looking out for him. He could see a black silhouette against one of the chequered panes. The figure moved back, and by the time Dan had signed into the visitor book and exchanged some comments with the on-duty assistant, Joe was settled back in the lounge. Dan walked across the threadbare floral carpet to Joe's seat beside the electric fire, drawing cold, fresh, outdoor air behind him.

'Well, this is a surprise!' Joe said, as if he didn't know that Dan always came this time every Sunday, as if he hadn't been looking out of the window in anticipation of Dan's arrival, as if it was unheard of that they should have tea and scones and play three games of Scrabble which Joe would always win.

Dan held out his hand and for a moment they sustained a quiet, motionless grasp, a facsimile of a vigorous man-to-man handshake. Joe's hands were broad and showed the history of his farmer's life; Dan could sense the effort his father was making to try to stop the tremor.

'How've you been?' Dan said.

'Same as.'

'Good,' Dan nodded. 'That's great.'

'Can't complain.'

Joe withdrew his hand. 'You ready to be thrashed then?' He picked up the Scrabble and shuffled purposefully towards the sun-room. He had taken to the game with the enthusiasm of the late convert, delighting in the obscure and arcane words thrown up by the Scrabble dictionary. Dan was happy to play. It gave a structure to their conversations; since the farm had gone, they'd lost the cycle of questions and commentaries that followed in the tracks of the farming year. They played Scrabble with a clock, because Joe, always eager to make his next move, became impatient with Dan, who dithered with his letters, working each tile as carefully as a rosary bead. Joe couldn't wait to get out to the farthest corners of the board, where all the triple scores waited.

With a glass roof and full height glass windows, and no

sunshine and no heaters, the room felt colder than outside. Dotted across the front lawn, rusty garden tables and chairs waited for a coat of paint and summer days. A tractor crawled along the boundary, headlights on, hard-cutting the hedges, throwing shredded Sycamore and Hawthorn up into the air. 'Left it a bit bloody late,' said Joe. 'I told them.' It was early spring, too close to the nesting season really for winter cutting. Dan wondered about the beetles and the ladybirds, He wondered whether the swallows had set out yet from Africa, and whether they would return to the farm and find a new place to nest amongst the burnt-out buildings.

'I went to the Council meeting,' Dan said.

Joe carried on turning all the tiles face down in the box.

'About the home. You know what's happened?'

'Course I do. They've been yapping on about nothing else all week.'

'So?'

'You going to pick up or not?'

'We need to talk about options.'

'Council said they'd find us somewhere else, didn't they?'

'Yes.'

'Can I go back to the farm?'

'No. You know you can't.'

'There you go then. What's to talk about?'

Sometimes Dan wished that Joe would come right out and blame him for the fire at the farm; tell him he should have done more, should have seen it coming, all the things that Dan tormented himself with. But he never had. Joe seemed, on the surface at least, to take the loss of the family farm with the same fatalism as a failed harvest or a lost ewe.

They played their usual three games; Dan came fairly close to winning one of them. The fog closed in around the deepening dusk, and they sat facing the invisible sea. Through the murk, the tractor's headlights in the distance made yellow spheres in the fog as the contractor tried to finish the hedge flailing. 'Rain forecast all through the next week,' Joe said. 'No way they'll be able to get onto the fields to do the inside of the hedges. No wonder matey's getting a spurt on tonight.'

Farmers live by the weather. It used to be predictable, but these last years had been unfathomable. Every year the winters had been milder, but so wet, the soil washing off the fields into burst-bank streams. When the flood defences of the harbour failed and the village was lost, they thought that nothing could be worse than that. They expected water to be their undoing on the farm, but it was fire that had finished them, that last hot, sleepless summer with the fields cracked like old china and all the pasture gone to dust. Fire had swept down from the tinder-dry moors right through, almost as far as the coast.

One of the kitchen staff stuck her head round the door and told them the tea trolley was on its way. She shivered and told them to get back in the lounge instead of freezing their whatnots off in the sun-room. But Joe made no attempt to move.

'We tried,' said Dan. 'I spoke at the meeting,' and he hoped Joe would realise what a step that had been for him, but Joe just said, 'It don't matter. I told you.'

At the meeting, they'd been shown a 3D model, complete with plastic families and plastic trees. The fate of the Home was cemented in a PowerPoint presentation: luxury apartments, penthouse suites, underground garaging; prime location, aspirational, lock-up-and-leave; swimming pool, restaurant, 24-hour concierge. While Dan stood and asked his carefully prepared question, the chairman walked his fingers through the model's high security gates and along the artist's impression of a herringbone brick driveway. The relatives and friends were reassured that alternative provision would be made.

'Don't make no difference where I live,' said Joe. 'Different if your mother was still with us, but she's not, so here, or somewhere else, it doesn't really matter. Long as we can still have a game of a Sunday, eh? Long as I can still thrash you at Scrabble.'

Dan hadn't even wanted to take on the farm, but Joe had moved to the shippen, promising not to interfere. His mother had already moved out by then. He wasn't a good farmer; his heart wasn't in it, and that's no way to run a farm. On top of the guilt about the fire was Dan's knowledge that the farm was well on the way to failing anyway. Joe would have seen that. It must have broken his heart, but true to his promise, he never interfered. Dan should have asked him for his help.

On the morning of the fire, that normal, boring, precious morning, Dan had been siphoning water from the kitchen sink into the butt by the door, trying to make their ration stretch a bit further. There'd been warnings before, of floods and landslips, and now fires in summer, so when he received the call, Dan ignored it and didn't bother about moving them to their evacuation point.

Dan had been out in the yard, fixing a gutter that'd been leaking for years, trying to get ready for the winter. He'd tasted the smoke in his tea before he smelt it. They had been lucky to escape with their lives.

'Don't miss that job,' Joe said, still looking out of the window at the tractor, hedging now in the dark. 'Not one little bit. Cars sitting on your arse, sounding their horns. Stop, go, letting the traffic past. Getting swore at. There was one time…'

'We'll miss tea,' Dan said. 'Come on.'

He tried to help Joe to his feet, but he pulled away. Joe pulled down his jumper, one of Rosie's hand knits, and too big for him now, baggy around the back and shoulders.

Dan opened the door to the lounge and was hit by a fug of

swampy, hot air that felt devoid of oxygen. They sat right by the fire, Dan amazed as always at his father's apparent insensitivity to temperature, hot or cold. There was a gentle scuff of cup against saucer, a TV in the next room, conversations in different corners, and Dan struggled to keep his eyes open. He nodded, jolted up, wide awake. Joe was looking hard at him. 'Keeping you up, are we?'

Dan looks at his watch. 'I'd better be...'

'I was thinking,' said Joe. 'Wherever I go next, I'd like there to be swallows. I like to think of them going all that way down Africa, then coming all the way back up again to exactly the same place.'

Dan wanted to say sorry. He tried to put his hand on his dad's shoulder, tried to reach out for some connection, but Joe evaded him, bending away from him to replace the Scrabble set on the shelf in the alcove.

'You mustn't worry yourself,' Joe said to Dan. 'It'll be alright.'

Joe lifted his hand, as if to say goodbye, or maybe just dismissing him. 'You'd better get yourself some practice in. Don't want to thrash you again, do I?'

ZERO HOURS
December 2032

Chloe Bolitho is caretaker and tour guide at New Lyonesse; zero hours, but it pays the bills. She rows small groups of visitors through a watery sky, over the hairdressers and the corner shop, over narrow lanes and smugglers' paths. She points out landmarks; the old sea wall, its benches now providing anchor-points for kelpy fingers that stretch towards the light; the car park with white-lined parking bays that appear and disappear with the tiding sand; and what little remains of her grandfather's house. Most of the old fishermen's cottages and the net lofts are already gone. It scarcely seems possible after centuries withstanding salt-laden air, but old lime mortar is quickly dissolved by acid sea.

Her visitors today are officials and dignitaries, come to see for themselves how the new memorial on the cliff looks from the water. There are clipboards, binoculars and folders, reference material, contracts and paraphernalia. The work is finished but until it's signed off and handed over, the official unveiling ceremony can't be organised, but the media have been given a provisional date to pencil in. Chloe rows them over the drowned village. The whole area is designated a maritime grave, protected from divers and the curious; boat access is controlled, and engine-powered boats are limited to a staid four knots, to minimise the risk of damaging the artefacts that lie so close to the surface at low tide. She notices that none of her guests look down to see what they are commemorating.

*

Banjo and Wes are both leaning against the cab of their

pick-up, enjoying the low winter sunshine that zig-zags across the wide spread of calm sea towards them. Banjo pours tea from a flask, sending steam into the cold morning air.

'Here we go,' says Banjo. 'The great and the good.' They watch the boat as it slowly progresses round the headland and stops.

Banjo waves. 'Don't be an idiot,' says Wes.

They've done their job as best they could, digging deep foundations for the memorial. The design competition was organised by a London firm, which also led the public consultations and the discussions with the funding bodies. There was call-out for the commission, which was awarded to a project mid-range in price and thought to be the least likely to offend anyone, although that could never be guaranteed. To everyone's approval, the artist was local, and the construction work was kept local too. The location was chosen, overlooking the sea, but stable.

They decided to recycle the inscription from the first glacier funeral in Iceland. It seemed fitting, and the committee couldn't come to an agreement on any of the other suggestions.

This memorial acknowledges that we know what needs to be done. Only you know if we did it.

Chloe holds the boat steady, while the visitors assess the monument, consult their plans, take photos of the cliffs, and the sea, and themselves, streaming straight to all their platforms.

Before the flood, whenever she wasn't working, Chloe spent a lot of time sitting on a bench on the harbour wall, just below where they are now. She'd thought exciting things happened anywhere but here, but she was never totally convinced and in the end she never left. Like all the girls, she went through a phase of wanting a mermaid's life, attracted by what she thought was their easy, iridescent glamour. A mermaid's fluke is tattooed neatly along the spine-fold at the base of her back, should she ever feel the need of it.

Chloe is a poet now, amongst other things, turning her hand to this and that, spinning her portfolio life to make a living. She still lives up on the new estate, in the same house, but the neighbours on both sides have moved away; there have been landslides and who wants to carry on taking the risk? Most of the houses are empty now, boarded up, waiting for some future, prosperous time.

*

Grace is walking along the coastal path. Just a walk; no objectives, no stone cairns to build, no world to save. It's difficult, but she's practicing, and trying to move on. She doesn't always succeed, and anxiety swamps her sometimes, but she tries to ride the ebb and flow, and she believes she's on the right track. As soon as she stopped her daily routine of collecting and building for one single day, there was the tiniest chink of belief that she could stop forever, without catastrophe. She doubts this with every fibre of her being and can't believe she's taking such a massive risk. But she is trying to at least pretend to be the woman she once was.

The coast path snakes up and down between dwarf windswept oaks and swathes of dry, golden bracken. As she approaches the crossroads of path and roadway, she sees Banjo and Wes parked up in the lay-by. Her first reaction is to hurry on, and pretend she's not seen them, but she forces herself to turn and walk up the slope towards their pick-up.

'Grace, good to see you,' Wes greets her with a wide smile. 'Shove up, Banjo.'

They shuffle along and make a space for her to join them, and she steps between them and leans against the pick-up.

'It's such a beautiful, beautiful day,' she says, and she can see that it is, and she means it.

'Tea?' Banjo reaches inside the cab for a chipped enamel cup. 'Sorry, it's not very clean.'

'That's fine,' she replies, and they stand in a line, enjoying the sunshine.

'We've done her proud,' says Wes, nodding towards the monument.

'They've asked me to unveil it,' says Grace. 'I had a letter.'

'Are you going to?'

Grace raises her hand to shield her eyes. She hasn't made a decision yet.

*

Chloe enjoys her work as tour guide, although visitors are few and far between and her position is always under threat. The Trustees talk about up-selling, and the importance of the tourist pound in supporting a new economy in this shifting place, where everything is unstable, nothing fixed.

She points out wildlife for the officials. It's been a good morning for bird sightings; there's was a puffin just off their stern for a while, difficult to see at first, until you knew it was there. On a normal tour, a sighting of something as exotic as puffins, dolphin or harbour porpoise means extra tips, as if she's responsible for making the arrangements and has conjured them up herself. Her tour group don't respond when she points out the puffin. The atmosphere has changed from politely collegiate to strained; there are tight voices, sighs, and juicy, fat silences. Chloe can't make out what's being said.

She can usually rely on a visit from at least one seal. They keep their distance, breaking the surface to survey the tour boat and its delighted visitors with their slow, close-to-human stares, before slipping below the surface to become shadows, curling and twisting around the streets like ghosts.

One of the visitors is getting energetically angry; holding up a drawing, he shows it to the others, and points, and compares, and someone else shrugs and turns away. Another man reaches over to the far side of the rowing boat to grab his rucksack full of papers, another stands up and sits down immediately as the boat sea-saws beneath him.

The puffin skitters away, keeping close to the waves. She wishes the officials would just take notice for a moment of something other than themselves.

She doesn't plan it, but Chloe stands up, practiced in not rocking the boat, and waits. The arguing voices falter and subside and they look at her, waiting for some sort of announcement. Her back tingles. She slips cleanly, noiselessly into the sea, and becomes a twisting, curling shadow beneath them.

Rewilding
March 2032

Caro always used to join in with the chatter and banter because there was really no choice, not in normal, everyday life. But she'd always tended towards the quiet.

During the first phase of the panic, there were online meetings, voices on voices, staggered stops and pile ups of words and stutters and silences. No-one noticed that she was the one who muted first, who clicked on a thumbs-up instead of speaking, who mimed her way through. And then the meetings fizzled out anyway, as the tech started to falter, and networks were commandeered for other purposes. Connections and nodes crackled and died. It was inevitable. It heralded the second phase of world-wide panic, when –

Dog-rose became eglantine, hawthorn became may, as weeks passed and the orders to stay at home came by megaphone from the sky. As months passed, her reversions continued. Honeysuckle became woodbine, aquilegia became columbine, and her language circled back on itself, rewinding, rewilding, her tongue becoming whole and wholesome again. The old words were easier on the tongue and gentler on the belly. She could stomach them and keep them down.

Caro stayed at home. She painted the ragged robin and cuckoo flower. She began to feel the length of the day-span instead of measuring it. There was time to harvest wild garlic, elderflower, wild strawberry and elderberry.

Sparrows colonised the wheel arches of the car that went nowhere. She'd always left windings of hair from her comb, out by the door for new nestings, but now she cut out the middleman and went direct, offering her shoulder for jackdaws and others to sit on and pull loose threads from her jumper, or take what they needed straight from her head. And if she needed to speak to a magpie or crow, why would she use her words? It was obvious. It was only natural.

She worried sometimes that she might lose words altogether, and if that happened, how would thinking be done? But it was worth the risk, and she liked her new life. She hoped that the change would be forever.

After the third wave, the panic subsided. It had been months – had it? – she wasn't sure how many. It was the planes coming back that told her it was over. She wept at the sky and the fresh vapour trails that bisected and straight-lined the blue.

Caro started to hear cars again, out in the distance, when the wind blew that way. Would they come to her? She wasn't ready. There was never much traffic down the lane, her lane, but still, the thought of people being able to drive past her cottage at any odd time, and suppose they stopped and knocked, people in cars, and asked for directions? What would she... what would she... would she be able to... If somebody asked, what would she say? People would ask, because anyone driving down her lane was going to be lost and needing directions to the nearest big place.

The first car was not lost people, but a van with the postman. A different one, it had been a long time and he wasn't to know.

He had thin, shiny papers about pizza deliveries and UPVC windows, all newly reopened for business. He knocked out of politeness, to let her know that normal was back. His eyes were black with sunglasses. She had to concentrate hard to decipher his words. She smiled at him and nodded, then shut the door, awkward and fumbling with shaking hands and sick to the pit of her stomach.

When she walked down the lane that evening, shuffling

through leaf-fall, there was a dead baby rabbit. Run over by the postman, small blood on the lane-way, its eyes widely open. She left it for jackdaws. Early next morning, she cut branches of blackthorn and laid them out across the lane. She didn't need much, the way was so narrow, more like a tunnel, dark with tree-shadows.

Blackthorn like needles for stitching leather. The postman's tyre flattened. He came on foot, knocked at her door, and she couldn't see his eyes again because of the blackness but she knew he was angry because of his loudness, even though she couldn't fasten on his words. She opened her mouth to make words back to him, but the words didn't come, and she was left standing in her doorway with her mouth wide, wide open but silent, as the postman walked away down the lane and –

It took time for her to close her mouth shut. Even after he'd gone. She just wasn't able. She wondered then whether it had all gone too far. Had her life slipped too far off its fulcrum to be retrieved? Was it too late to unlock and re-engage her voice? But she felt no need to rejoin the cumulative noise of the world, or to add to it in any way. Even if she could. There was no going back, and she wondered how many, like her, had found other, new, better ways.

Sometimes Caro still opens her mouth, just to see what will happen but she can't – she just can't – push the words out. Not even the old words, the ones that were easier on her tongue and gentler on her belly, the old words she could swallow and keep down in her body.

ABOUT THE AUTHOR

Jackie Taylor is originally from London but has lived and worked in rural Cornwall for the past twenty years. She has several jobs and writes when she can, mainly short stories and poetry. Her short stories have appeared in various publications, most recently in Mslexia and the *Stories For Homes 2* anthology, as well as in *Dusk, Tymes Goe By Turnes* and *No Spider Harmed in the Making of this Book* for Arachne Press.

About Arachne Press

Arachne Press is a micro publisher of (award-winning!) short story and poetry anthologies and collections, novels, including a Carnegie Medal nominated young adult novel, and a photographic portrait collection.

We are expanding our range all the time, but the short form is our first love. We keep fiction and poetry live, (although on-line, at the moment) through readings, festivals (in particular our Solstice Shorts Festival), workshops, exhibitions and all things to do with writing.

All our books are also available as eBooks, and this year, with the assistance of Arts Council England, we are branching out into audiobooks, for most of our 2021 titles, including this one.

https://arachnepress.com/
Follow us on Twitter: @ArachnePress @SolShorts
Instagram: @ArachnePress
Facebook: ArachnePress SolsticeShorts2014